DARK IRISH

AN O'BRIEN NOVELLA

STACEY REYNOLDS

Raven Of The Sea: An O'Brien Tale
A Lantern In the Dark:An O'Brien Tale
Shadow Guardian: An O'Brien Tale
Fio: An O'Brien Novella
River Angels: An O'Brien Tale
The Wishing Bridge: An O'Brien Tale
The Irish Midwife: An O'Brien Tale
His Wild Irish Rose: De Clare Legacy

This book is dedicated to my readers. I thank God every day for you.

CHARACTERS FROM THE O'BRIEN
TALES SERIES

Sean O'Brien- Married to Sorcha (Mullen), father to Aidan, Michael, Brigid, Patrick, Liam, Seany (Sean Jr.), brother of William (deceased) and Maeve, son of Aoife and David. Retired and Reserve Garda officer. Native to Doolin, Co. Clare, Ireland.

Sorcha O'Brien- Maiden name of Mullen. Daughter of Michael and Edith Mullen. Sister of John (deceased). Native to Belfast, Northern Ireland. Married to Sean O'Brien with whom she has six children and eight grandchildren. A nurse midwife for over thirty years.

Brigid (O'Brien) Murphy- Daughter of Sean and Sorcha, Michael's twin, married to Finn Murphy. Mother to Cora, Colin, and Declan.

Finn Murphy- Husband to Brigid. Father of Cora, Colin, and Declan. I.T. expert who works in Ennis but does consulting work with the Garda on occasion.

Cora Murphy- Daughter of Brigid and Finn. Has emerging gifts of pre-cognition and other psychic abilities. Oldest grandchild of Sean and Sorcha.

Michael O'Brien- Son of Sean and Sorcha, married to

Branna (O'Mara), three children Brian, Halley, and Ian. Rescue swimmer for the Irish Coast Guard. Twin to Brigid.

Branna (O'Mara) O'Brien- American, married to Michael. Orphaned when her father was killed in the 2nd Battle of Fallujah (Major Brian O'Mara, USMC) and then lost her mother, Meghan (Kelly) O'Mara to breast cancer six years later. Mother to Brian, Halley, and Ian. Real Estate investor.

Capt. Aidan O'Brien, Royal Irish Regiment- Son and eldest child of Sean and Sorcha O'Brien. Married to Alanna (Falk). Father of two children, David (Davey) and Isla. Serves active duty in the Royal Irish Regiment and currently living in Shropshire, England.

Alanna (Falk) O'Brien- American, married to Aidan, daughter of Hans Falk and Felicity Richards (divorced). Step-daughter of Doctor Mary Flynn of Co. Clare. Mother to Davey and Isla. Best friend to Branna. Clinical Psychologist working with British military families battling PTSD and traumatic brain injuries.

Patrick O'Brien- Son of Sean and Sorcha. Married to Caitlyn (Nagle). Father to Estela, Patrick, and Orla. Currently residing in Dublin after joining the Garda. Serving on the National Security Surveillance Unit on the Armed Response Team.

Caitlyn (Nagle) O'Brien- Daughter of Ronan and Bernadette Nagle, sister to Madeline and Mary. Married to Patrick. Mother to Estela, Patrick, and Orla. Early education teacher. English as a second language teacher for small children. Native to Co. Clare.

Estela O'Brien- native to Manaus, Brazil. Adopted daughter of Patrick and Caitlyn O'Brien.

Patrick O'Brien Jr.- Born in Dublin, Ireland. Adopted son of Patrick and Caitlyn O'Brien.

Orla O'Brien- daughter of Patrick and Caitlyn O'Brien.

Dr. Liam O'Brien- Second youngest child of Sean and Sorcha. Internal medicine and infectious disease specialist. Married to Dr. Izzy Collier.

Dr. Isolde (Izzy) Collier- Doctor/Surgeon recently separated from the United States Navy. Married to Dr. Liam O'Brien. Born in Wilcox, Arizona. Close friend to Alanna O'Brien. Daughter of Rhys and Donna Collier.

Sean (Seany) O'Brien Jr.- Youngest child of Sean and Sorcha. Serving with the fire services in Dublin. Trained paramedic and fireman. Unmarried and no children.

Tadgh O'Brien- Only son of William (deceased) and Katie (Donoghue) O'Brien. Special Detectives Unit of the Garda. Married to Charlie Ryan.

Charlotte aka Charlie (Ryan) O'Brien- American FBI Agent with the International Human Rights Crime Division. Married to Tadgh. Sister to Josh. Currently working in Europe as the liaison to Interpol.

Josh O'Brien- Formerly Joshua Albert Ryan. Brother of Charlie. Attending junior college for Maritime Studies and living with Sean Jr.

Dr. Mary Flynn-Falk- Retired M.D., wife of Hans Falk. Stepmother to Alanna O'Brien and Captain Erik Falk, USMC.

Sgt. Major Hans Falk, USMC Ret.- American, father of Alanna and Erik. Married to Doc Mary. Retired from the United States Marine Corps.

Daniel McPherson- Son of Molly Price and Jonathan (John) Mullen. Sorcha's nephew. Just recently found the Mullen family. Was an unknown offspring of John, who never knew he had a son. Raised in the Scottish borderlands by his English mother. Molly Price married an old friend who claimed Daniel as his son.

Maeve (O'Brien) Carrington- Daughter of David and

Aoife. Wife to Nolan, mother to Cian and Cormac. Sister of Sean Sr.

Katie (Donoghue) O'Brien- Native to Inis Oirr, Aran Islands. Widow of William O'Brien. Mother of Tadgh O'Brien.

David O'Brien- Husband of Aoife, father of Sean, William, and Maeve. The oldest living patriarch of the O'Brien family.

Aoife (Kerr) O'Brien- Wife of David O'Brien, mother of Sean, William, and Maeve. Originally from Co. Donegal.

Michael Mullen- Native to Belfast, Northern Ireland, married to Edith (Kavanagh). Father of Sorcha and John.

Edith (Kavanagh) Mullen- Married to Michael Mullen, mother of Sorcha and John.

Madeline Nagle- Caitlyn's sister, daughter to Ronan and Bernadette Nagle.

Mary Nagle- Caitlyn's sister, daughter to Ronan and Bernadette Nagle.

Miren O'Donnell- Finn Murphy's aunt.

Aideen (O'Donnell) Murphy- Finn's mother.

Jenny- Daytime barmaid at Gus O'Connor's Pub.

Dr. Seamus O'Keefe- an OB-GYN who met Liam and Izzy in Brazil.

Genoveva Maguire- an orphan from St. Clare's in Brazil who now lives with her natural father, Quinn Maguire, in Ireland.

CHAPTER 1

DOOLIN, CO. CLARE, IRELAND

*F*inn Murphy was a patient man. It was part of the job, so to speak. Anyone brave enough to take on Brigid O'Brien and enter into the realm of wedded bliss had to have a bloody Ph.D. in patience. "For the love of the Virgin, Brigid. Move your ass! We're going to be late!" Brigid made an appearance out of their first-floor master, and it was like getting knocked over by gale-force winds. "Wow." He breathed the word like a prayer.

She smiled, doing a little twirl. Ten years of marriage, and she still stole his breath. "Worth the wait?"

He stalked toward her, suddenly not in such a rush. "We can skip the ceremony. The only fun part is the reception."

She laughed as he slid his arm around her waist, pulling her tight to him. "Oh, no. Your sister would never forgive me. I'm supposed to do a reading!" She squealed as he palmed her ass.

"Give me five minutes. That's all I need."

"Yes, you're a man. But if you're going to mess up my hair and make-up, I'll need more than five minutes from you. Now let's go, love. It's an hour to the church."

Finn knew she was right. "Raincheck, then. I'm going to have to insist on a raincheck and at least an hour of your undivided attention..." he looked down as he paused, "while wearing those shoes."

She was dressed as fresh as a daisy. Her frock was simply lined and cotton. A pinafore style dress, which was reminiscent of the 1950s or '60s. It was blue and had sprays of flowers with green foliage and red blossoms. The shoes, though, were candy apple red. High and sexy, making her look tall for once in her life. Usually, she came up to his sternum. Now she was up to the top of his pectoral muscle and looking like prim and proper sin. Little white gloves, a green handbag, and her auburn hair falling in smooth waves down her back, draping her shoulders. He looked into her eyes, remembering their own wedding day. Those blue-green eyes which looked so much like her twin's but at the same time, uniquely hers. Full of mischief and a hidden sensuality that was for him and him alone.

Brigid ran a hand up Finn's forearm, feeling the familiar pull that hummed between herself and her mate. She thumbed the tattoo inside his forearm. A new one. The first one anyone could see. The rest were for her eyes only, unless they were at the beach or he was with family and shirtless. His hair was unbound, which was unusual. He usually kept the midnight hair bound at his neck. It came to the top of his chest and was thick and silky. "We may need two hours," she said, giving him her best come hither stare. "Maybe your mam can keep the kids one more night."

"Now, you're talking," he said with a rakish grin. "Consider it done." He swept a soft kiss over her lips, then he took her hand and led her out the door.

* * *

SLIGO ABBEY, Co. Sligo

Cora ran among the abbey ruins, letting her cousins and brother chase her. She could outrun them, of course, but where was the fun in that? What kind of cousin or sister would she be if she didn't give them a sporting chance? She came around a stone structure, slamming into a solid body. She squealed as the figure growled and picked her up, swinging her around. "Uncle Josh!" She threw her arms around his neck, delighted at her unexpected captor.

"Hello, sweetheart. How's my Cora?" Josh said. His Yank accent was strange to her ears, after having not seen him for months.

"What are ye doing here? I didn't know you were invited. Do ye know my auntie?"

"No. I'm crashing. Shh," he said as he put a finger to his lips. He put her down, and they walked. "I was hunting for a job and a place to live, since Seany and I have a mind to move west. I was staying with Granny Katie in Galway last night and decided to stop and say hello."

"Is it true you're going to volunteer for the lifeboat and go to school?" Cora took his hand, walking through the old abbey. "Uncle Tadgh said you like the water."

"I do, and I need to find work. I didn't..." He thought about how to phrase things with Cora. "My parents didn't have money to send me to school." He sat on an old flat stone, and she sat beside him. "I've got to make my own way. I've got to go to work and school, so I can keep my student visa."

Cora put her head on his shoulder. He loved the girl like a little sister. She was a sweet, sensitive child, and too smart by half. "I hope you can stay here forever. I don't know much about visas other than they can be taken away. Auntie Branna would have had to worry about it as well if she hadn't married my uncle."

Josh smiled at that. "Yes, well, I don't have a Michael to marry. Or Michele in my case."

"If they send you off, I could marry you when I'm older. Mam's got a book like that. One of those romance novels Auntie Alanna gave to her. *A Marriage of Convenience*. I'll marry you when I'm eighteen, and then they can't take you away from us."

Josh held in his laugh because he didn't want to hurt her feelings. "That's a very kind offer. I'm afraid I'll be an old man by then. You should marry someone your own age who loves you the way a man loves a woman."

"Oh, I know all about that. It seems like a bunch of nonsense to me."

He grinned at that. "But you're an O'Brien. Don't you want to find your mate like your mother did?" he asked.

"Well, you're an O'Brien now. It's the same for you. You've got a mate somewhere. Ye've just got to keep an eye out. The rest of my uncles made it more difficult than they needed to. Look at Seany. Granny says she might never get a grandchild out of him."

Josh barked out a laugh. "Too right. Well, if you find a potential mate for me, you let me know. I'm afraid I have had pretty poor luck up until this point."

"Ye're lookin' in the wrong places. Sometimes what you need is right in front of you. It's like that with Da when he can't find his keys. Sometimes they were right under his nose."

"You are way too wise to be nine years old," Josh said with a smile.

"Aye, it's the sight. Granny Aoife says I have an ancient soul. Grandda Dónal says it's my selkie blood."

"I've heard the story. So, your grandad on the Murphy side thinks you're a selkie?"

"Not exactly. It's like we've got traces of the blood, but we can't shapeshift or anything. Now that would be grand! I'd like to be able to shapeshift. I'd be able to swim faster than Jenny McBreed. She's the captain of the junior swim team. Her father is the coach, and she thinks she's some sort of royalty. I tried out for the team, but I wasn't quite fast enough. I mess it up on the flip turn."

"Well, coming from a lifelong swimmer, I'll tell you that you've got to train hard and often. You don't have a lot of public swimming pools near you. I could work with you if you like. Once I'm living on the west coast, I'll work with you. I can guarantee you that your times will improve, and you'll make the team next year. We can't let that Murphy selkie blood of yours go to waste."

"Oh, it's not the Murphy side or the O'Donnell side. It's the McDubh side that has the dark hair and eyes. That's what the name means. Black ones. It's not a common last name. Some say we're descended from the Picts, north of Hadrian's Wall. The ones that lived near the coast of Scotia. I don't know, really. I seem to be the only one with the sight."

"It's a gift, Cora. You should never be afraid of what you can do," Josh said kindly. "I envy you." He was amazed by this child. Beautiful in an otherworldly way, like she'd been brushed by the fairies. And she was wicked smart.

She said, "Sometimes, it makes me feel alone, being the only one." Her voice was quiet, but then she looked up, and her face lit from within. "Hello, Da! Josh is going to teach me to swim faster when he moves here. And we're going to practice my flip turns."

Josh noticed Finn was staring hard at Cora. He looked almost sad. But it's likely how a parent would feel if they had no way to protect their child from the world, or from the loneliness which often plagued extraordinary people. He greeted him, giving him an understanding look.

Josh tugged a stray curl from her dark mane. "Soon, you'll

be so fast in the water, little miss Jenny McBreed will eat your bubbles."

* * *

GALWAY, Ireland

Madeline Nagle sat across from her student advisor, trying hard to rein in her temper. "It's simple, Phillipe. All I need you to do is sign off on that little piece of paper, and I'm home free. I don't need the credits, and it's a waste of my study time."

"Part of your course requirement demands you be in the field. That's for Celtic Studies and Humanities. You must actually interact with real people in a professional setting. By doing this assignment, you'll kill two birds with one stone."

"I've documented…"

Her advisor held a hand up. "Glorified people watching. It's not enough. Hence, the field trip," he said plainly.

"What is taking a group of students on a tour of Inis Mor going to prove to you, Phillipe?"

"If you are going to do more with these two degrees than roll into a doctorate, you need to get out of the library and use your knowledge with actual human beings," he said, not able to hide the French accent even though he'd lived in Ireland for five years.

"Actual humans stare into their phones and take selfies off the side of the boat," she said with a dry tone, which said exactly what she thought of this assignment.

"Then give them a reason to look up." He gave her a very Gallic shrug and pushed her proposal back toward her. "If you do this weekend excursion in two months, I'll sign off on your thesis proposal. This project will take two semesters if you work around the clock. It's a huge undertaking with minimal outside help, given the nature of your work. You can start next August session, as long as I sign on the dotted line. So, give me a reason to say yes." He stood, walking out of his office. "It's teatime. Just remember, the water is rough in autumn. Bring your raincoat and a jumper. Maybe some sea sickness tablets."

She bristled at that. "I'm a Nagle. I don't get seasick. You French lot could learn a thing or two from the Irish."

He smiled at that, not taking offense. "It was good to see you again, Madeline," he said as she mumbled and grumbled her way to the exit.

Madeline went to the student great hall at the National University of Ireland- Galway and searched the crowd for her sister's blonde head. It wasn't like she could call for her. Calling out the name Mary in a public forum in Ireland was likely to get about a hundred responses.

Mary waved, and she joined her. "You're late. How did it go? Did he go for it?"

"No, not yet. He has a condition," Madeline said grimly. Then she explained.

Mary waved a hand in dismissal. "Christ, girl. That's a piece of cake."

Madeline gave her a sideways glance. "For you, maybe. It's ghastly altogether if you're in my shoes."

"You always were quiet. Unless you are close to the person, I mean. Just try to pretend they're old friends or cousins. And you're actually passionate about the subject matter. This isn't a hardship, Maddie. Just pretend they're all Josh O'Brien."

Madeline almost jumped out of her knickers. Her eyes shot to Mary's. "What are you on about? I..."

Mary put her hand up. "Don't even start. Ye've got stars in your eyes whenever he's around. If it helps, I think he's into you. He tries very hard not to be, which is insane, but I think the feeling is mutual."

Madeline picked at her cuticles. "Don't tease me, Mary." But Mary wasn't teasing.

CHAPTER 2

DOOLIN, CO. CLARE, IRELAND

One Week Later...

Finn hovered over his woman, feeling her arch. The lamp on the bureau lit up her face as she strained against him. She was pinned beneath him, his hands shackling her wrists just like she liked it. Hard and dominant. She might be a spitfire for the rest of the world, but in bed, she liked it when he didn't hold back. Liked his big body and feral, dark features as he took her hard. Not always, of course. Sometimes she climbed on him like a she-cat. She liked to straddle his hips and ride him. He liked it too. Loved it. She was the wee sister of the O'Brien clan, but she was a little demon in the bedroom. "I need more. Fuck!" He pushed his knee up and spread her wide, tilting his hips. Then he cut loose, driving deep and hard. She arched under him, her head going back as she released around him. She stifled her cries so no one would wake, and he felt her teeth in his chest. The orgasm tackled him and shot up his spine. There was no muffling him, though. He growled as he came.

Brigid watched her beautiful husband in the dim light of the bedroom. They both preferred the light on. Liked to watch each other. She didn't want to miss anything. He was magnificent. He'd let go of her wrists, propping on one arm as he lifted her hips. Wanting to get closer and deeper so he could fill her up. His black hair shined like a panther's pelt in the light. His bronze skin and tattoos writhed as his muscles rolled. Breathtaking.

In the aftermath of their lovemaking, she gave a contented sigh. Sprawled across his broad chest, she kissed his smooth skin. He was one of those rare men who didn't have at least a dusting of hair on his chest. The fine hairs were soft and barely detectable. It made his tattoo unobstructed. He tasted salty from their sweat, but it wasn't unpleasant. He smelled good. He had an earthy, male scent which only condensed after sex. His hair smelled delicious.

Finn ran a light finger from Brigid's neck, down the expanse of her spine. She was soft and ivory, and he'd never tire of feeling her all warm and spent from his loving. She was the single best thing that had ever happened to him. It was this contentment that made him miss the warning shot of a migraine until the tendrils started clawing up the back of his head and over to rest in his eye socket. He grabbed his head and moaned.

Brigid cursed, "Oh, Jesus! I'll get the light." She turned the light off within a second. "I'll get a compress." She threw her robe on and ran out of the bedroom and into the kitchen. When she came back with the icepack she said, "Finn, it's never hit you this fast. What can I do?"

Nothing, he could tell her. "Just get the meds." Even though they didn't really help. At least, they knocked him out. It was better than nothing. Just as another wave of pain went through his head, he heard muffled cries. He stiffened, his eyes blurring as he looked out their door into the lighted area of the kitchen. "Cora," he croaked. "Go to her. Something is wrong." His words were rough. Brigid hesitated.

"Go, love. I'll get the meds. Go to her. She shouldn't be alone."

Brigid left and his head fell back on the pillow. Cora didn't have these episodes often, but when she did, it was upsetting for her. For them too, because they couldn't protect her from them. If he could, he would. He thought back to his own childhood, and pushed the thoughts away. He heard a knock. Luckily he was covered, because his aunt would have gotten a hell of a good post-coitus view of him otherwise. "I'm okay, Auntie. It's just another migraine."

She went to the bathroom door. "Where are your meds, Finn?"

"In the right cupboard. Thanks." He heard her rustling around, then filling the glass he kept by the sink. She pressed the glass into one hand and handed him a pill. "There now." He took it with some water, and she took the glass. She rubbed the hair off his face like he was a boy. "My poor lad. Still trying to keep those demons at bay, aren't ye?" She didn't say anything else when she felt him stiffen. "I'll go check on the lass."

* * *

CORA SHOOK in her mother's arms, trying to shake off the feeling of darkness which surrounded her. She was so cold. So very cold and wet...or maybe not. She assessed herself, fingering her nightgown. Not wet. But the dream had seemed so real. "I was in the water. I was so cold and the swells kept coming. It was pulling me fast. I was being drawn through the water, away from everyone. And it was so cold and grey." She was crying, and her mother tried to soothe her. "I want Da. Where's Da?"

"He's got one of his headaches, darlin'. I'm sorry. What can I do?" Cora opened her eyes stiffened as she saw her great-aunt in the doorway. She barely knew this aunt, but something was so familiar about her. She had silver hair, but there were remnants of the black hair of the McDubh side of the family. She looked rather like a lovely, aging witch. "Auntie Miren, is my da okay?"

"He's going to be just fine, love. It's just a…well…it's a sort of tension headache. He's had them since he was a lad. He wasn't much older than Colin when they began."

Brigid's hand stilled on Cora's head, "He never told me they went that far back. He's only been getting them for about six years."

Miren shrugged, "I suppose he must have had a remission of sorts. Now, my dear Cora. Tell me more about this dream. Was it just a bad dream or was it a vision?"

They were both surprised at her candor. Finn's own mother didn't like talking about Cora's gifts. She'd never said as much, but she always found a way to change the subject. Apparently not so with this strange, ethereal creature who had stayed with them after Colleen's wedding. Cora asked, "You know what I can do?"

Her aunt walked into the room, and she took a seat on the edge of the bed. "Aye, Cora. I know. It's just, I don't know how it works for you. From what I've heard, it can be different for people. Is it always dreams?"

Cora's face lost some of the tension. Instead of answering her aunt, she asked another question. "Do you know more people like me?"

Before her Aunt Miren could answer, Brigid interrupted. "Finn Murphy, you should be in bed!"

Cora started a fresh wave of tears, "I need you, Da. I'm sorry about your head, but…" She was hiccupping as her emotions began ascending again.

He looked like death. He was pale and covered in a sheen of cold sweat. "I'm here, mo leanbh." *My child.* He looked at

Brigid, giving her a weak smile. "I'll sleep with her. The meds will have me out in no time." Then he gave his aunt a strained smile. Something flashed in his eyes, and then it was gone. Something like a gentle warning. She stood. "Get some sleep, lad. Then tomorrow, I'll take you to breakfast. Just like when you were little."

Cora cocked her head, questioning. Finn said, "Your Great-Aunt Miren used to make your grandmother nuts, because she'd take me out for breakfast and stuff me full of sweeties." His voice was strained, trying to sound light-hearted, but it was taking a toll.

Miren said, "Aideen was always a killjoy." But when Finn gave her another chiding look, she stopped at that. Aideen and Miren had made a tentative peace in recent years, but there had been a time when they weren't on speaking terms. Finn had been young when the rift occurred. Maybe four or five years old. But that sort of thing made an impression, and he'd felt the absence of his favorite aunt keenly. The two sisters had finally come together and made a promise to forget the old hurts, right after their mother had passed. Miren had always been a bit different than the others. Like him, the dark Irish genes were dominant. She loved the sea and saw too much when it came to people. Especially her nephew.

Brigid pulled the covers back, tucking Finn into bed like a boy. She killed the lights, and she brought his icepack and water into the room. Her heart squeezed as he stifled the moan of pain which threatened at the base of his throat. She kissed both their heads. "I'm glad you aren't going to work tomorrow. This one hit you fast, Finn. I think I should call the doctor."

"Bring me a pail, love. I'm not sure my dinner is going to stay put."

"Maybe you should come back into our room. I think

Cora's okay, Finn." But he was already drifting off in a medicated haze.

Miren watched Finn's lovely, fierce wife leave the bedroom. She kept the door cracked so she could hear if either of the two occupants needed her. Brigid gave her a sad look. Miren said, "It's hard to watch them suffer; isn't it? Both in their own ways."

Brigid said, "Yes, it is. But they're a united front. You'll never meet a finer father. He's always the first at her side when the dreams come. Except for tonight. Tonight, the headache came on him suddenly. It's got me a bit worried."

"He'll be fine, love. He's had brain scans. Full workups. It's hard to watch, but it'll pass. Now, how about some tea? I'd like to talk to you about something."

Brigid made the tea and slid a cup to her aunt-by-marriage. She liked Miren. She was unconventional. Unlike her mother-in-law, Miren was more of a free spirit. She wore long skirts and flouncy blouses. She wore her black and silver hair loose and long instead of a more polished look. It was strange to have her here. She'd heard about her, but for some reason she stayed away from the family, living in isolation in the midlands. Her recent retirement was the only reason she was here for an extended stay. As a pensioner, she was free to wander. "What is it you wanted to talk about?"

Miren answered, "About an extended stay. Now that you have a guest cottage next door, I want to rent it for the winter. I'll clear out when tourist season starts."

"You can stay as long as you like. We bought it as an investment, but also for family. We don't have a guest room anymore, and we'd love to have you. It would be easier than using the boy's room and having them on the pull-out." As if on cue, Colin stirred on the sofa bed, then settled again.

"I'd insist on paying rent. I've been looking to sublet my flat until my lease is up. I'm tired of the midlands. I need to get back to the sea. I'm out of sorts being so landlocked. I'm retired now. I don't need to be in Tipperary anymore, and honestly, I never liked it there. Full of chancers and travelers." Brigid knew what she meant. Not tourists. Travelers were gypsies, and they caused a lot of trouble. Mostly theft, but they liked a good brawl as well.

"I can't blame you there. We got our car broken into in Tipperary, and good luck getting the guards to show up that far away."

"Yes, well now that I'm retired, I'm washing my hands of the place. I wouldn't be terribly troublesome. I'd just like to spend the winter looking around the coast for a good property. I could help you with the children. I know your mother has gone back to work."

"Aye, she has. She just caught another local baby this week. I think it's a grand idea, Auntie. And Finn will be over the moon. Consider it done."

Miren squeezed her hand. This was perfect. She was needed here. They didn't know it yet, but she did. She'd seen it clear as day.

* * *

DUBLIN, Ireland

Josh woke to the sound of the front door opening. A spike of anxiety went through him as he grasped for full consciousness. It was always this way after dreaming of home, or what used to be home. He shot out of bed, trying to escape the claws of the dream. Well, not completely a dream. More of a memory which ebbed and flowed, blending with the fiction that was summoned by his sleeping mind. His father's angry voice slurred with drink. Then Charlie screaming. He, hiding in his room like a coward. But unlike the memory, other memories which weren't as clear came back to him. His mother's muffled cries from their bedroom. Pleading of a sort that he hadn't understood until later in life. Marks on his mother's neck.

His father was a monster. Always had been, really. A violent drunk, and in hindsight, probably much more. Josh couldn't think about what had gone down behind that closed door. What his drunk father had done against his mother's will. But the whimpering pleas haunted his dreams now and again, and the wave of despair that consumed him upon waking was enough to buckle his knees.

He practically ran into Seany as he opened the bedroom door. Sean Jr. was the youngest of the O'Brien brothers and his new best friend. He was more like a brother, really. "Christ, Josh! You look like shit."

"Thanks, honey. I love you, too," he croaked the words, giving a weak smile.

Seany wasn't fooled. "Ye had another nightmare; didn't you?"

"Yes. You were doing the dishes in a tutu and your fireman's hat. It was horrifying."

"I'm serious, Josh. Maybe you should try talking to the counselor again. PTSD isn't just for soldiers and cops. Alanna knows about these things. They're back in Belfast now, she and Aidan. Maybe I could…"

"I'm fine, Sean. Don't go saying anything to Charlie. I'm fucking serious, dude. I don't need a shrink." He was being assessed for permanent citizenship. No one needed to see him as a mental health issue or a drain on national health care. No doctors unless he paid for it, and he didn't have the money.

Seany put his hands up in defeat. "Okay, okay. How did your final go?"

Josh smiled, glad for the distraction. "I aced it, of course. Did you doubt it?"

"You are a cocky bastard. So, that's it. You've finished your two-year degree? What's next? A bachelors?"

"I can't afford it. Waiting tables part-time is paying the bills, but not much extra. I've applied for the apprenticeship with the Navigation and Maritime Services. So, we'll see. I need to keep my student visa going until I'm working full-time. The pay is shitty, but I think it's considered an internship, so I'm still considered a student. At least that's how they explained it to me."

"Well, it sounds like you've got your bases covered. When will you find out?"

"Any day now. Listen, I mean it about Charlie. She can't be worrying about this stuff so far along in her pregnancy. They just got settled in the new house. I don't want to add any stress to either of them."

"You know Tadgh would help you, Josh."

"I know he would, but I need to stand on my own two feet. I'm an adult. I don't want to burden them."

Seany narrowed his eyes. "You are not a burden, Josh. To any of us."

"Is that why you pay more rent than me? Because I'm such an asset?" Josh hated that he was bringing so little to the table.

"You are helping me. I'd never be able to afford the rent in Dublin if I wasn't bunking in with you. It's one of the reasons we're moving. And I didn't want to live with a stranger. I'm not putting down roots in Dublin. When we move, you'll be able to afford half the rent and we'll have our own rooms."

"Thank God. I don't know how you O'Brien's crammed two and three in a room. The dirty socks alone would make it a hazmat zone."

"True enough. I did know where they all hid their girly magazines, though. I got an early education." They bantered back and forth as Seany made a late-night snack. "I got word about the transfer, tonight."

Josh dropped the remote before he'd even turned on the television. "Why the hell didn't you lead with that? What's doing?"

"Galway City, where the grass is green and the girls are pretty," he said with a rakish grin.

"Nice! We'll be near Tadgh's mom and grandparents!"

Seany laughed. "Only you would think of that first. No thought of college girls or the pub scene."

"Yeah, well I've got you to be my social director. I'm new to the big family thing. You take it for granted. I'm thinking about granny's homemade cookies and free laundry facilities. I'll renew the job search now that I have a county to narrow it down. And I'm going to register with the Royal National Lifeboat in Galway County. It should look good with the immigration people; right? That isn't why I'm doing it, but still. Michael said he'd grease the wheels for me. I think Tadgh's old motorcycle and Liam's old car should suffice between the two of us; don't you think? Hell yeah!" He was getting more excited by the minute. "Get me out of this frigging city. I've had enough concrete jungle to last a lifetime. I cut my teeth on Urban Rust Belt America. Galway sounds fucking perfect."

"Aye, well Galway City's rent is a bit dear as well. We'll have to look out of the city a bit. Maybe an old cottage that needs some work."

"Sounds good to me, brother. I have lived in some downright hovels. A fixer-upper cottage would have been a step up."

Seany's heart squeezed in his chest. He hated to think about the fact that Charlie and Josh had been reared in a hovel with a violent father. He'd like to beat the hell out of that father of theirs. "Okay, Galway it is. I'll tell my boss it's a go. I didn't want to commit until we talked."

"Galway it is. When is it happening?"

"Sixty days. I think you should go ahead and let me finish up here. The sooner we find a place to rent, the better. You can go ahead as soon as you find a place and find work."

Josh headed back to bed when Seany said lightly, "You know who's at NUI Galway don't you? In the Humanities department."

"Seany," Josh's tone held a slight warning. "Don't start."

"Oh, I'll start. I'll keep going until you pull your head out of your ass. I know you like her, Josh. What I can't figure out is what the hell you're waiting for. Maddie's great. Girls like her don't stay single."

"Christ, you talk about Aunt Sorcha hounding you to settle down. You're just as bad. Madeline is great. Both the Nagle girls are. They're just not for me. Madeline wouldn't look twice at someone like me, and that's a good thing. She deserves better than some kid out of the Cleveland ghetto."

"I can't believe you just said that. What the hell does that make Charlie? You know, your amazing, successful sister who came out of the same household?"

"Charlie is different. She's the best of us. I am who I am in spite of my father. Decent enough, given the example I had. But she is who she is because of him. She's strong because she had to survive him. She had to protect me. I'm not half Charlie's equal. It's just different."

"It's not different, Josh. And Madeline Nagle is not as immune to you as you think she is."

"You're crazy. Just drop it. Okay? I'm going to bed. I'll start job hunting first thing in the morning."

"Okay, I'm right behind you. I'm knackered. We trained hard today. I'm skipping the run tomorrow."

"Me too. Sixty days is not a lot of time to relocate, but I got this. You just concentrate on work. I'll do the rest."

Josh went to bed, trying to imagine living outside a major city. Not to just visit, but to be on that gorgeous west coast for good. The Wild Atlantic Way, they called it. And it was wild. Rocky shores, spongy bogs, heather and foxglove blooming in the summer. Sea spray on solitary lighthouses. It was more than he'd ever hoped for. They'd have family and friends nearby. Good people who cared about him.

He thought of Seany's words. *You know who's at NUI Galway don't you? In the Humanities department?* Of course he knew. He pictured Madeline Nagle with her ashy blonde hair and her grey-green eyes. A beautiful, sweet face and a husky, musical voice. Yes, he knew exactly how close in proximity he would be to the quiet, intelligent woman, and it would break his heart.

CHAPTER 3

*C*ora took the biscuits out of the oven, laying the tray to the side to cool. "Auntie Miren, can I ask you something?"

"Yes dear, anything." She winced at that, however, because it wasn't altogether true. She couldn't tell her anything and everything.

"What was my da like as a boy? He talks about when he was older, but I never really hear much about him when he was a wee boy. I know he played football and the violin. He got good grades. I know how he met my mother at university. I just…I always feel like there's a big blank space. Even grandmother doesn't talk much about him when he was little."

Miren had to tread carefully. "Well, let me think. I don't remember all that much. I came and went, ye see. He was a beautiful boy. He looked a lot like you. He was very sensitive."

"How do you mean?"

"Well, he just felt things deeply. He had the migraines

when he was younger, too. But they cleared up later. I was gone for it, but I was glad to hear it."

Miren took a sip of tea just as Cora shocked the shit out of her. "Why doesn't he know you're psychic?" Miren spit her tea out onto the table linen, coughing and sputtering. Cora hid a smile as she took a sip of her own.

Miren narrowed her eyes. "How long have ye been waiting to drop that little nugget?"

"I've known for sure for a couple of weeks. My visions are more regular, and ye seem to be around right when I need you. Like we're…"

"Linked," Miren finished.

"Are we?" Cora said, tilting her head.

"I think we are just more in tune to one another because of the bond we share."

"So why doesn't Da know?" Cora sounded so sincere. She really did have the utmost faith in her father.

Miren measured her words, because she was no liar. "Your grandmother isn't comfortable with the subject. And like I said, I moved away."

That seemed to satisfy Cora for a time.

"Has the vision shown you anything else?" Miren asked, changing the subject.

Cora said, "No. not yet. It's just cold and wet. I can taste salt. It's dark, but not nighttime. I'm being pulled. It's fast, and I'm cutting through the water. I can't see anything clearly. It's like there's water in my eyes. It's so cold."

"I'm sorry if it frightens you. I'd help if I could."

"I know you would. It'll come eventually. It usually does. I'm not afraid for myself. It's my uncle." Cora's eyes became haunted. "I've already talked to him. He said he'll take extra care at work."

"Would that be the uncle in the Coast Guard?" Miren knew she had many uncles.

"Yes, Michael. And now my uncle Josh is signed up with the National Lifeboat. It's got me in pieces, Auntie. I hate falling asleep."

"Well, you have to sleep, my love. My experience is that fighting your gifts rarely ends well."

"Is that what you did?" Cora asked. "Did you fight it?"

"Me? No. Mine come to me differently. I'm not asleep. It's during times of great relaxation I channel. I've learned to control them and even bring them on. It comes with time, and everyone is different. All that said, I think my mother, your great grandmother and my sister, would have preferred that I tried to suppress the visions. It scared your gran, because our mother, your great grandmother, was convinced it must be some sort of abomination against the church. It's one of the reasons I've never lived nearby for long. That sort of talk made an impression on your gran."

"She never told me she thought I was an abomination." Cora said sadly.

"Oh, Christ. Child, that's not what I meant. She never thought that in the way our mother did. She doesn't think that about you. Our mother was a closed-minded woman. She never understood. I think your gran just feels helpless with all of this, and she can't understand it so it scares her. But she doesn't think it's evil. She never thought that. I'm sorry. I sometimes forget you're only ten."

"One more day until I'm ten. Mam is picking up my cake from Granny's house. Great-Granny Edith is visiting, so it'll be beautiful. They can all bake, but Edith is the one who likes to decorate."

"Any theme in particular? Barbie? Disney?" Miren was happy to have changed the subject.

"Harry Potter. I'm a Gryffindor like Hermione."

"Can't say that I've read them. I'll have to give them a try this winter, when the fire is warm and the chilly weather comes." As if on cue, the autumn breeze came through the window of the cottage, leaves rustling outside. "October birthdays are fun. Who's coming tomorrow? Any friends from school?"

Cora shrugged, "No. I decided I'd rather have a family party. My friend from Dublin is coming with Liam and Izzy. Her name is Genoveva. She stays with Caitlyn so she can see her sister. I mean, it's kind of her sister. They were in an orphanage together in Brazil. Would ye like to walk with me, Auntie? I'll tell you all about it. I have to check on the neighbor's ewe. She got hung up in some fencing. She's calmer when I help and she needs her bandages changed. I'm good with animals, I think."

"That's wonderful. Animals are pure and innocent. You're dark Irish. You're connected to the natural world in ways other people aren't. Let's go meet this ewe of yours."

* * *

THE BLACK ROSE (*ROISIN DUBH*), Galway, Ireland

Josh nursed his Smithwicks and played with the droplets of condensation on the glass. Seany had stepped out the front door to answer a phone call from work. He was nearly ready to transfer into his next unit here in Galway. They had just moved into the old converted barn they now called home. It was farther up the coast in a small village. The downtown area of Galway was not convenient to the average person driving into Galway City. Mostly due to the lack of parking. Roisin Dubh was walking distance from the fire station, which would pay off in a couple of weeks. For now, they'd parked at the Donoghues row house, Tadgh's maternal grandparents. The walk was far, but the parking was free.

The craic was good at Roisin Dubh. Fewer old village men and more people their own age. NUI Galway fed a steady stream of university kids into the pubs. The barn was a bit rough around the edges, but once they cleaned it up and painted, it would do nicely. They had their own room, and Josh could afford to pay half the rent. Na Forbacha, or Furbogh, was a small village with little to offer. It did, however, have small boat access, which made his work with the National Lifeboat easier. Seany's commute to the fire station was minimal, so the location of the cottage was good for both of them.

Josh thought about the last two years and could scarcely even fathom where his life had taken him. He'd gone from being a senior at a public high school in Cleveland, living in a dive apartment complex, and dodging blows from his angry, drunk father, to being emancipated and moving to Ireland. He'd changed his name, been adopted by an amazing family, and started college. He'd never left the greater Cleveland area in his first seventeen years. But now, everything was different. He'd stood inside ruins older than the Egyptian pyramids. He'd kayaked in sea caves with seals swimming under his boat. He'd begun studying the life, culture, and technology surrounding the oceans. He'd started picking up a little Gaelic. He had a new best friend. Actually, more like a brother. A voice came from behind him, smokey and feminine.

"Are ye going to nurse that one pint all night, or are ye game for another?"

Josh turned around to find a very attractive, dark haired woman behind him. Very dark-haired. The out-of-the-bottle kind. But still, she was a looker. She had an edgy look to her. Dramatic makeup, a top that came above the waistline to show a belly ring. She wasn't his normal type, but she had a pull. That wasn't true, actually. She reminded him of a girl he'd dated in his junior year of high school. Darlene Jennings. He answered her. "I'm afraid you'll find me rather boring. I'm a one-and-done kinda guy." Thanks to his father's violent drinking tirades, he wasn't much of a drinker.

"Cute and a Yank? Well, I suppose you'll have to buy me a drink then." She sat uninvited, but he wasn't going to be rude. Seany would certainly give up his seat for a lady. He motioned to the bartender who gave the woman a glass of cheap red wine to replace the one that was almost empty. She was slim in her snug jeans and sandals. Thin and long-limbed. Her eyes were icy blue and intense. Almost predatory. He thought of another woman with muted, grey green eyes. A woman who was this woman's opposite in every way. He took her in anew. Yes, a bit predatory. And maybe tonight, he felt like being prey.

CHAPTER 4

DOOLIN, CO. CLARE

*B*rigid pulled the icepack from the freezer and switched the phone to the other ear. As she turned, she almost dropped everything. "Jaysus, Miren! Ye scared me half to death."

"I am sorry. I knocked." Without even looking at the icepack, she said, "It's Finn, is it? Yes, you speak to the doctor and I'll take this to him."

She didn't wait for a response. She took the icepack and bottle of tablets out of her hand and started down the hall to Cora's room. She wanted to test something. She peered in. Cora was asleep. She'd been in bed with a fever for two days prior and her sleep schedule was off. Hence, the nap in the middle of the day. It was Saturday, so everyone was home. She turned back around to tend to Finn, passing by Colin and Declan's room. They were playing Mario Kart and completely oblivious to the troubles. She went into Finn's room.

He groaned and she felt a pang of guilt. She really was the worst aunt that ever drew breath. But her suspicions were gone. "There there, lad. How's my boy?"

"Morning, Auntie." Finn was really such a sweet lad.

"It's the afternoon, love. You're all turned around, aren't you? How long has this one been going?" She laid the icepack on his head and waited for the answer. She already knew the answer, but she wanted to hear him say it.

"About an hour ago," he croaked.

"A few minutes after putting the wee girl to bed, was it?" She really shouldn't be so fat headed about the whole thing.

"How did you..." He paused, as if calculating something through the fog of pain. "Auntie, you better start talking. I'm just in enough pain to forget my manners. What have you been up to?"

She smoothed the crinkle in between his eyes and rubbed his forehead. He went lax on the pillow, deciding to cooperate. "Just testing a theory, love. I started meditating about an hour ago. You know how I get when I go in deep. Right around the time Cora fell asleep. So, you say that's when the migraine started?"

He sat up, the icepack sliding down his bare back and causing him to squeak. He took it in hand and gave her a harsh stare. "What have you been playing at, Miren?"

"Oh, Miren is it? What happened to Auntie? Aren't you in a bad way. And before you give me that look, no. I didn't say anything to your lovely wife. Cora has known for some time. Do you know why, my darling nephew? Because she feels a pull when I'm near. She feels a sort of connection. She asked me if we were linked. She said the dreams started in earnest when I moved next door. Have your headaches increased, Finn? And don't you dare lie to me."

Finn cursed under his breath, dodging the question. "What did you tell her, Auntie?"

She heard the doorbell. What she hadn't expected was the voice. Well, well. Aideen was back from Switzerland. Finn said curtly, "We'll talk about this later."

Miren looked over her shoulder to see her sister. As lovely as an Irish rose. She was petite. Her figure had softened over the years, but she was still just as pretty. Silver hair that had changed from the warm brown brown of her youth, and pale, blue eyes. She was the light to Miren's dark. Blissfully ordinary and happier for it, no doubt. She watched Aideen tense as she took in the sight. She stood up and moved away from Finn, knowing that was the cause of her unspoken distress. She didn't even know she did it. Aideen was a killjoy. That wasn't a lie. But she wasn't cruel. She loved her children. She protected them the only way that was available to her. Just because she'd been wrong a few times, it didn't mean she wasn't a good mother. "Hello, Aideen. How was Switzerland? Are the men as pretty and ill-humored as I remember?"

The corner of Aideen's mouth twitched upward. They'd spent the summer of their twentieth and twenty-first years backpacking in Germany, Switzerland, and Austria. Miren far preferred the lake district in Austria. Hallstatt was an ancient Celtic settlement. The place had a unique energy in its soil. In the deep recesses of the salt mines, the mountains, and the rich earth that covered the banks of the lakes. The Hallstätter Sea was pure magic all year round. Deep, cold, and placid, it held power. But then again, she'd always been drawn to water. And in her twenties, she had a flare for the dramatic. She'd had a fast and furious affair with a young carpenter. By the end of the week, he'd been ready to propose marriage, but she'd broken his heart and left for Switzerland. Her sister had felt sorry for the lad, but Miren had been young and impossible to tame at that age.

Her sister gave her sister a kiss and hug, and Miren eased a bit. She smelled the same. Exactly the same. The wedding had been so chaotic they'd barely spoken. Miren had arrived that very day. Then, Aideen and her husband left for holiday soon after the wedding, and he'd gone on to Singapore for work. Aideen was used to caring for someone, and having the last child marry and her husband out of town must have her feeling lonely. She said, "Retirement looks good on you, love. A month in the Alps sounds like heaven."

Aideen turned, speaking over her shoulder. "You'd have hated it. No water for miles. Now, what's this I hear about another headache, my lad?" She leaned over and kissed Finn who was drifting. She instinctively used her lips to check his temperature. "Is it the same thingCora had? Do ye have the sniffles?"

"No, Mam. It's just an aching head. No bother."

Brigid spoke from behind them. "They've been coming back-to-back. The doctor can fit him in next week."

"I don't need a doctor, hen. I need a couple of tablets and some sleep. Come rub my head and stop pecking at me."

Brigid squirmed in beside him and against the wall. Aideen smirked. "I've been replaced. It's the fate of all mothers, I suppose." She watched with humor as Finn nuzzled against Brigid like a big cat while she grazed his scalp with her nails.

As she closed the door behind them, Miren said, "They are happy; aren't they? And the children," she put her hand to her breast, "they are wonderful. You are lucky, Aideen. I have friends whose grandchildren would rival the demons right out of Dante's Inferno." Her sister chuckled. "That said, we best not go too far in case the children get up and about. Tea or coffee?"

They settled in with tea and biscuits while the household stayed still. But the peace didn't last long. Twenty minutes later, Aideen was on her feet. "Aideen, please don't walk away from this. I'm not blaming you."

"You are! You do blame me. How do you even know for sure? These headaches..."

"Almost stopped completely when I moved. Am I correct?" Aideen was silent. Proof enough. "And they started back up again when Cora was about four years old. I'd wager that's when…" But Aideen wouldn't let her finish.

"Stop it, Miren. I can't do this with you again. I won't. I'm glad you're here. We've all missed you. But I won't allow you to start digging up things that are long buried."

"That's what you don't understand, Aideen. You never did. Some things weren't meant to be buried."

* * *

NA FORBACHA, Co. Galway, Ireland

Seany cringed as he walked out of his bedroom to find Josh's bad idea staring at him from the kitchen table. Justine McNamara was not Josh's type, and Seany couldn't fucking believe she'd latched herself onto his brother like a bad germ. She was a regular at the pub, a messy drunk, and calculating. Josh deserved better. There was something about this woman he didn't like. She showed up when he and Josh were out. Even at the Salthill promenade when he and Josh were running. Sean spent his days off in Galway. He hadn't transferred to the Galway station yet. One of the men in Dublin went on unexpected leave when his wife went into premature labor. It left them shorthanded for a month and he was needed.

He'd been there when Josh met Justine. He thought it was a passing flirtation. Josh wasn't the type to do an empty one night stand. But then he'd ended up going home with her, and now she was like shite on a shoe. In the last two weeks, she'd made sure to monopolize Josh's free time. She smiled at him. "Good morning, Sean. Good to see you." He buttoned his shirt, not liking her appraisal of his bare chest.

"Good morning, Justine. Is Josh awake?" He knew Josh

had to work in two hours, and the kid needed this job. Josh had done a summer at the ferry dock in Doolin when he first moved to Ireland. Now, one of the Galway ferry lines had given him a part time gig for the fall and winter schedule. Josh had a competitive swim background and volunteered for the National Lifeboat, so he was a good man to have on a boat during a winter crossing. His other job was at the *Pie Maker* in Galway City. Smallest restaurant in the country, damn good fare, and constantly had a line out the door. Josh already had a fan club of young uni girls that fought for a table during lunchtime. Not surprisingly, Justine tried to get him to quit and come work at the pub near her. But there was no way Josh was going to work at a bar with his family history. He didn't like drunk men. Too bad he didn't have the same aversion to drunk women.

"He's awake," she answered. "I've got to run. I'm sure we'll see each other later." Seany cringed. He really didn't like this woman. She hadn't actually done anything. She just seemed to stalk Josh with her eyes. Always assessing. He was going to have to talk to Josh about it. When he'd thought it was a one and done, he kept his mouth shut. But she was so manipulative. Inserting herself in everything. And the worst part was that Josh didn't even realize what he'd done. He'd bandaged over his feelings for Madeline by seeking out the complete opposite. Maddie was quiet and serious and naturally beautiful. She was intelligent. And she saw Josh. She really saw him. She listened. If he wasn't careful, he was going to miss an opportunity at the real thing by busying himself with this pub rat.

He looked up as Josh made an appearance in the doorway. He blushed when Seany made eye contact. He actually flushed with embarrassment like a school boy, which solidified the notion that Justine was absolutely the wrong woman for him. She sauntered over and kissed Josh with inappropriate thoroughness. She said, "What's the matter, pet? Surely you're not shy about a little kiss." Josh discreetly detangled himself and went to the coffee pot. "Morning, brother. When do you head back?"

"Tomorrow morning," Seany answered. "I thought we could go to dinner at your grandparents' house before I head back. Katie is cooking her stew. You know, just the family." The look he gave Josh made his point clear. No Justine.

"That sounds perfect. I'm off at two." The air positively buzzed with Justine's irritation. She got her purse, her coat, and gave a curt goodbye.

Josh looked exhausted as he watched her leave. Once they heard her car pull away, Seany let it rip. "What the hell do you see in her? She's not for you, Josh. You have to know that."

Josh took a sip of his coffee. "It's not serious. She just came off a bad break up. She's looking for some company. So am I. It's not a big deal."

Seany shook his head. "You don't see how she tracks your schedule? Shows up uninvited? She's already sleeping over a couple of nights a week. You don't even know her, Josh."

Josh turned his back, mumbling something to appease Seany. Then Sean froze. "Josh, is that blood on your shirt?" The fabric was actually stuck to his skin, like the blood had seeped through and dried. Josh turned around.

"It's nothing. A branch or something." But Seany wouldn't be put off.

"Then you need to clean it, at least. You'll never reach it on your own. Sit down." He was getting into his first aid kit before Josh could argue. "I mean it. Sit the fuck down." Josh's shoulders slumped, and all sorts of alarms were going off in Seany's mind. He started easing the shirt off, careful with the part that was stuck to his back. It opened up the wound a little. Seany just stared dumbly, the shirt still in his hand.

Then he said, "I don't want that little bitch in this house anymore."

Josh tried to stand up and Seany put an arm on him. "Jesus, Sean! Like you haven't had a little rough sex before?" Even as he said it, Seany saw the blush come back to his face. This hadn't been his idea, obviously.

The nail marks were more than just a set of crescent nail marks during the throes of passion. She'd raked all five nails across his back for a good five or six inches. And he had a bite mark on the cap of his shoulder. Bruised and angry where she'd actually broken his skin. "If it was just a bit of rough sex, why did you lie? Did you leave marks on her?"

"Hell no! I would never!" Josh sounded genuinely offended.

"Exactly. Yet you'll allow this to be done to you? These are deep and they're deliberate. You need to end it with this woman. I didn't say anything at first, but I don't like her."

"I have this under control, Sean. Just leave it alone. Justine isn't all bad. She just had a little too much to drink and got over zealous. I'll talk to her about it. It won't happen again. Just drop it, Sean. Seriously. This is my business." But as Seany disinfected the claw marks and bite wound, he whole-heartedly disagreed. You hurt one of them, you hurt all of them. That was how O'Briens worked. And Justine had to go.

* * *

One Week Later
National University of Ireland, Galway

Madeline walked down the outdoor strand connecting the buildings at the university. The quadrangle entrance shaded her for a brief moment and opened into the green expanse inside the structure. It was a warm day, the ivy showing different shades of green, red, and orange. She could spot her sister in any crowd. Her golden locks were bright in the sunlight, and she was waving like a lunatic. Then there were the surrounding lads. Always at least three. Today there were five young suitors, all with stars in their eyes. Mary couldn't help it. She attracted them with her energy as much as her looks. A pang of affection squeezed Madeline's heart. They were close in age, Madeline being older by a little more than a year. Mary was her best friend and her better half. Mary ran forward and hit her like a missile, hugging her tightly.

"Come meet my study group. Lads, this is my sister Maddie." The names slipped through her mind like sand. She was terrible with names. She remembered the essence of a person more effectively. The guy with the shifty eyes. The girl with the dimples and infectious laugh. Names took at least three meetings. These five guys only gave her a cursory glance before focusing on Mary again. Hot females were a commodity in the engineering wing. Electrical and Computer Engineering was a sausage fest. So, when one of the co-eds had Mary's looks and brains, the nerds swarmed her like a collective hive. She dealt with it gracefully but dated outside her own species. She was on the tail end of an amicable break up with a medical student. He was too busy, and she was too time consuming. Or something like that. The way Mary put it, the guy wanted an easy shag in between test weeks, and she was being a prude. He was looking for the less complicated and more physical. And despite Mary's easy grace, she had depths that some tosser at NUI was not going to fully appreciate.

It made Madeline proud that her sister had walked away from what could be considered a good "catch" for a college boyfriend. She heard Mary make her apologies and dismiss the fan club, and she turned to her. "So, do you have your tour and talking points ready for the big field trip this weekend?"

"Aye, I do. I didn't manage to weasel out of it. Phillipe is a hard nugget."

"I wish I could go, but this test is going to be tough. I've assessed the competition, as you can see. A couple of them are straight up geniuses. The others are passably smart. But this is a contest. I'll bat my eyes, they'll assume I'm a diversity plant, and I'll hand them their asses when I crack the code first."

Madeline laughed, slinging her arm around Mary's shoulders. "I swear I can't fathom how we sprung from the same womb. Ye make me feel like a moron when you let your geek out in full force."

"You aren't a moron. You're bloody brilliant, Maddie. Just in a different way. I could never do what you do. All the history and theories. And your Irish is flawless. They've been teaching it to us since we were in nappies and mine never came out so smoothly. Thank God I had you to help me study for the yearly exams. Now, I've just rung off with Seany O'Brien. We're invited to meet the family out at the pub. They're up north a bit, along the coast. Some little village pub in Furbogh. And don't tell me you have to study, because I know you're lying. You need a night out. And the Murphy's will be there, so I can talk to Finn about that internship."

"Who else is coming?" Madeline tried to keep her tone light, but Mary knew her too well.

"Tadgh and Patrick will be there. Michael and Branna as well. Probably several children and grandparents. You know the O'Briens." She decided to let Maddie off the hook and come out with it. "Seany's off work. His transfer was delayed a few weeks for some reason. He seemed to think Josh needed a night out with his family. He said the cottage is shaping up nicely. What do you say, Maddie? Come with me?" It's only about 90 minutes back home. I'll be the designated driver."

Madeline hated how much she really wanted to go. "All right. I'm in. Let's get some tea. I have to submit some notes from the library, but I'll be done by six. Just meet me in the carpark."

CHAPTER 5

FURBOUGH, CO. GALWAY

*M*ichael laughed quietly as his youngest brother showed him the hot water main for the cottage they'd just painted. The outside looked great. The family was together. Boys will be boys, as the old saying goes, and that additional bit about all work and no play had them looking for mischief. Finn, Patrick, and Tadgh were right next to him, all snickering like ten-year-olds. Josh was in the shower. The women were in the sitting room, completely unaware. At least, they thought so until Brigid poked her head into the dry rotted door, making Finn squeak like he'd been caught. "What are you all up to?" Then she looked at Michael's hand on the water turn off. She'd been the victim of this particular trick more than once when she took too long in the shower. "Ye're always trying to leave me out of the fun!"

Michael hissed at his twin. "Then shut your wee gob and have a listen. You're going to blow the whole thing!"

Brigid stuck out her tongue at him. She was in her mid-thirties, but her twin brought out the devil in her every time. Michael put a finger to his lips to shush the rumble of laugh-

38

ter. Then he started to turn quickly. In seconds the hot water to the house was shut off. They hung in silent anticipation. And waited. Any minute now Josh was going to give a yelp because the shower had turned to ice. The plumbing was fed from a spring, and the water was deadly cold.

Then the voice came from behind them. "You boys are losing your touch." And, then it hit. A bucket of ice water came first, and then the garden hose. They were trapped. Stuck in the crevice behind the cottage that housed the plumbing. They'd either have to trample wee Brigid or suffer the assault of Josh's garden hose. That's when Tadgh flew into action. He picked Brigid up by the elbows, put her in front of them like a shield, and they marched out in single file. Brigid was squealing like a little hellcat while Cora, Estela, and Michael's twins Halley and Brian cheered from the sidelines. Branna, Caitlyn, and Finn's Aunt Miren stood frozen in awe with babies on their hips. Josh, refusing to continue to hammer poor Brigid, dropped the hose and ran like the devil was after him. It was all fun and games until Josh's only piece of covering...a bath towel...caught on a piece of fencing.

* * *

MARY WAS LAUGHING SO HARD, soda water was trickling off her chin. Madeline was trying not to laugh. Really. But the whole thing was just so...She put her head down and shook with contained giggles. "I see you over there, Miss Madeline. It wasn't funny at all!" Brigid's indignant tone would have been more believable if she hadn't been trying so hard not to laugh as well.

Tadgh said, proudly, "And I thought the fine, manly parts were genetic, but our adopted baby boy made a good showing."

"Good? Good? Try spectacular!" Josh said with bravado, but his pink cheeks betrayed his embarrassment. He risked a look at Madeline, whose quiet, smiling eyes warmed him to his toes.

Her sister Mary was not shy, however. "Do tell. A good showing, was it?"

Cora interrupted. "Yer all a bunch of perverts. I had to hide the little ones' eyes, and my own. And poor Josh ended up begging for his towel from behind a tool shed." Which led to another rash of giggles.

Miren watched the young people banter back and forth and just smiled contentedly. Finn's wife was a little spitfire, as feisty as she was pretty. She felt her nephew approach. "Did you need another white wine, Auntie?"

"Not at all. I'll be nodding off like an old woman if I have another. I shouldn't have had the haddock and chips." She looked around. "So Caitlyn is the one that Cora told me about. The one who'd had no children, and then three within less than a year?"

"Yes, that's right. Caitlyn and Patrick adopted Estela and Patrick Jr. and then had little Orla just last month."

She looked over at Patrick who had a baby boy on his knee. Caitlyn had a tiny newborn strapped to her chest and a little girl who looked about four who never left her side. Big, brown, soulful eyes and a beautiful, caramel complexion. Then her eyes lit on the younger two Nagle sisters again. One was golden blonde with the same bright eyes as Caitlyn. The other was more of a muted blonde with deeper colored eyes, but no less lovely. Truly remarkable, as a matter of fact. But that wasn't what drew her eye. She felt a niggling at the back of her brain she would need to revisit later. Not now, of course. Her relaxation techniques weren't subtle, and she didn't want to corner the lass on her first meeting. Still, there was something. She looked at Cora and to her astonishment, the girl was looking at Madeline as well. Her brow furrowed, she started to rub her arms like she'd caught a chill. Finn noticed it as well. When he moved beside her, he pulled her close as she started to shake.

Josh reflected that Madeline Nagle had never looked better. It was a crime she seemed to get prettier every time he saw her. *There was no help for it*, as Grandma Katie would say. She was just too good to be real. She was genuinely sweet and wicked smart. He watched her head turn as if someone had tapped on her shoulder. Finn and Cora were behind her. That's when he saw it. Cora shivering like she was sitting on an iceberg. He stood at the same time Madeline said, "Cora, love. Are ye catching a chill?" Before anyone could argue, she took off her jumper and knelt before the child. Brigid and Miren were the next wave of a growing crowd of family that had noticed that their beloved Cora was in some sort of distress, and then Finn started rubbing the back of his neck. Madeline slid the sweater over Cora's head.

"I'm sorry. I don't know what's wrong. I just feel cold," Cora said. "It's nothing at all."

Brigid felt her forehead. "She's not warm. Still, it looks like you and your da could use some rest."

"I don't want to go. I feel okay." But the shaking didn't cease.

Madeline said softly, "I'll tell you what. You keep that jumper, and I'll come visit and bring you some toffee from a shop near my school. Ye like toffee, right?"

Cora nodded, curling into the warm jumper. "Thank you, Maddie." When they got up to leave, Josh knelt down and took her hands. Cora hugged him so fiercely it almost knocked him down. "Be ready, Josh."

He cocked his head. "Ready for what, sweetie?"

"I don't know, but you will. All I know is you should be ready."

41

* * *

SEANY LEFT RIGHT after his sister and her brood, needing to get back to the Dublin apartment they had possession of for another week. After that he'd be sleeping at the station until he left for the new one. As it was, he was sleeping on a lone mattress they'd be throwing away after he left for good. He had one bowl, one fork, flatware for one, and a sleeve of paper cups. He also had their crappy microwave. Station food was manna from heaven compared to the pot noodles he'd been surviving on the last few weeks. As he drove back to Dublin, he thought about his sweet Cora. He hoped to God she wasn't getting sick. They needed a good streak of luck in the O'Brien family. Especially where the women were concerned.

Between the abduction of Alanna, the tragic death of Eve, and almost losing Izzy, the O'Brien women needed to lie low and behave. How terrifying it must be to have a mate. He'd thought, long ago, about having one. The folly of youth, no doubt. A summer romance and the sting of first love and then loss. He'd spent years trying to forget about Moe. To be free of the childhood infatuation. Had it been love? He didn't know. All he knew was that given the relationships which surrounded him, he would never settle. And that kept him single. Probably best, really. He was only twenty-one. Then again, with the looks that were crossing the room between Maddie and Josh, his new best mate could very well be married before him. He'd take the idea of Josh marrying young over Josh letting that crackpot Justine hang on any longer.

* * *

MARY NAGLE GROANED INTERNALLY as Josh said an awkward

goodbye. Her sister was an utter fool. He was gorgeous altogether, and he liked Maddie. A lot. Any fool could see the undercurrent of attraction between them. Her sister had always been more of a loner. She had a small circle of friends, and she was more bookish than anyone she knew. But she was loyal and felt things very deeply. That is, when she let herself.

They paid their bill and the waiter said absently, "Don't forget your mobile."

That's when she looked over and saw it. Josh's mobile was sitting on the bench seat. "Maddie, isn't that Josh's?"

Maddie gave it a glance and said, "I think so. And Sean has gone to Dublin. He'll need his phone. He's with the lifeboat."

"We need to take it to him. Text Caitlyn and get his address." Mary picked up the phone and saw several notifications. "Someone's been trying to ring him."

His phone was buzzing on silent mode. Madeline said, "Don't snoop, Mary. The house is just up the road. Let's go. I've got an early class." Madeline was a teacher's assistant for one of her favorite teachers. It was a lot of work, but she paid Maddie a small wage.

"Too right. Such a pity that we'll have to see the dashing, young Yank with regularity. Hopefully he's in a towel again," Mary said as she wiggled her brows at Madeline.

Madeline didn't need reminded of that story. Picturing Josh in nothing but a towel was bad enough. Without the towel was too much to bear.

* * *

WHEN JOSH PULLED into the narrow gravel drive on the motorcycle, he groaned. It was bad enough it had started drizzling, but as the headlight lit up the front of the cottage, a bad feeling washed over him. He said evenly, "Justine, what's up?"

"What's up? Could you sound more like a feckin' Yank? What's up is that you're screening my calls."

He exhaled, suddenly too tired to deal with her. She'd been to the pub, no doubt. She hung with the Galway townies, not the university crowd. Then what she said to him sunk in. He started patting down his pockets. "Shit! I left my phone at the restaurant."

She handed him her phone. "Just ring them. They'll hold it for you."

He had his burner phone from the Lifeboat if he really needed to make a call, so he decided it was best to call the pub directly. He used her phone as they both walked in the house. No answer.

"They've likely closed up for the night. You won't get it 'til morning."

"You're probably right." He put his keys on the hook and then checked that his phone for the Royal Lifeboat was fully charged.

"You didn't answer me, Josh. Why didn't you pick up when I called and texted?" Justine asked pissily.

"Justine, I was having dinner with my family. I don't play with my phone when I'm with them. We talk. No one checks their messages or Facebook. You'd get to know people better if you put down your phone once in a while."

"Was it just family?" Jesus, Josh thought. She was really giving him the third degree. Maybe Seany had a point.

"Justine, I'm really tired. I told you I was busy tonight, yet you have gone out of your way to make a problem where there wasn't one." He saw the barely contained anger in her. It gave him a sick feeling. Almost like déjà vu. The house was full of tense energy. Then she was on him, kissing him hard and causing him to balance himself against the wall. He didn't want this. He didn't understand her. She palmed his cock, however, and his will started to weaken. Then he thought about their last coupling. She'd been so rough. Scratching and biting him seemed to drive her into a bone bending orgasm. He tried to please her, but she always wanted something more. A bigger piece of him.

The decision about whether to let Justine throw him down and ride him senseless was interrupted by a knock at the door. Just in time, actually, because he'd just pressed his hips forward, letting her get a good feel of how hard he was. He was so weak. He disgusted himself. Definitely just in time. Justine swore. He walked to the door, pulling his shirt tail down to cover his erection. He'd never have guessed who it was in a million years.

"Madeline, Mary, hello. Please come in out of the rain." Josh's guts dropped into his boots. Justine eyed the two pretty women with a predator's gaze.

Mary handed the phone to him, giving Justine the side eye like she was waiting for her to pounce. "You left it on the bench."

"Thank you. I just called and didn't reach the restaurant staff. I really appreciate this. Would you like something to drink?" Josh felt like he'd been kicked in the nuts. Why the hell had Justine shown up at the worst possible time? He hated that they'd caught him with a woman at his place.

He looked at Madeline. Her cheeks were flushed pink, her eyes not meeting his. "No thank you. We can see you have company."

He nearly smacked himself. "I'm being rude. Madeline, Mary, this is my friend Justine."

Justine visibly bristled at the title. Madeline, however, was the picture of good manners. "It's a pleasure, Justine. We're sorry to intrude."

Mary interrupted. "I forgot to ask you, tonight. How did the long job search pan out?"

Josh smiled, "I have three jobs. I'm working at the Pie Maker, the ferry, and interning with the Commissioner of Irish Lights. One of their contractors, actually."

"I guess it helps to be an adorable Yank. Everyone wants to hire you! Well, then. We'll be off back to Doolin. Mam and Da never sleep until we're home."

Justine's tone was sickening and sweet, which meant she was being a bitch and barely trying to hide it as she said, "Ye both still live with your parents? How cute you are."

That's when Madeline showed the first flicker of backbone. "Aye, we do. Coming from a loving home is a blessing to be sure. Nothing I need to make excuses about." When she said it, she watched Josh flinch just a bit and wished she could take the comment back. He hadn't come from a loving home. She didn't know his story, but she knew that much. She finished, "Josh knows all about that. He's an O'Brien and they show up in force when he needs them." He blushed and gave her a grateful smile.

Josh said, "That they do. Are you sure you can't stay for a cup of tea?" Josh wanted them to stay, and he didn't. He did want Justine to leave, however. How had he gotten in so deep with her in such a short time? She was integrating herself into every aspect of his life. The girls made their apologies and headed out the door. When he turned from the door, Justine's arms were crossed. "Family, huh? Try again."

"They are family. By marriage and distant, but family."

"Which means nothing in your case because you aren't a real O'Brien anyway. Are you shagging either of them?"

"Jesus, Justine. That's beneath even you. And it's honestly none of your business. We never discussed being exclusive. You can do as you please. Right now, I think you should leave. I'm tired, and you are out of line." He opened the door, showing her the way out. She stopped in front of him and palmed his cock again. "Who's going to take care of this? Surely those two can't handle you."

He pulled her hand away and stepped back, not meeting her eyes but keeping the door wide open.

She hissed at him. "Fuck you!"

CHAPTER 6

COMMISIONER OF IRISH LIGHTS-
NAVIGATION AND MARITIME SERVICES-
EERAGH LIGHTHOUSE

*J*osh's head was buzzing with nervous energy and excitement. He walked along the stone base of the lighthouse, loving the look of the structure. Tall and powerful, it had served these waters for just over two hundred years. His old, crusty companion smiled. "This one has had many lives and custodians. Technology changes the way things work, as you know. Starting with oil lamps, then electricity. We've seen wind power give way to solar. But the bones of this place are old and wise and deserving of our respect. Some of the more remote lighthouses like this one still need an attendant. Too temperamental to leave on their own. Sometimes I swear these old lighthouses get lonely. At least this one isn't a hotspot for the tourists. Damn annoying when they're taking pictures while you're trying to work."

Josh laughed at that. "Then I will not confess my own guilt in that regard."

"It's not many men who think to go down this path. It's all power suits and MacBooks™ now; isn't it? This is just as specialized. It takes a sharp mind. But it also takes the sort of lad who doesn't mind the seawater seeping into his trousers. Are you ready for this? I'll teach you everything I know, but if you don't like the harsh elements or the solitude, this may not be the life you want."

"Seawater and solitude suit me just fine, Mr. Dawley. And I appreciate it. I'm excited to learn from you. More excited than I've ever been about anything."

"Call me Pete. Mr. Dawley makes me feel old." He clapped his hands and said, "Well then, let's go into the belly of the beast, shall we?"

Josh was embarrassed to be a little winded by the time they reached the last step. Too many Sunday roasts and lemon cakes. The wind was whipping at the top. Pete said, "The weather's turning. Some series of hurricanes messing up the Atlantic. They say it's not going to hit us, but we'll feel it just the same. Big swells and high winds. You keep that Lifeboat mobile with you. Between your job at the ferry, this job, and your volunteering, I think you're going to have an eventful week. You might want to tell that pie shop to ease up your schedule."

"Yes, that's a good idea. Although, the tips are pretty good. I thought you all didn't tip over here, but I'm making a killing."

Pete's eyes sparkled with mischief. "Oh, yes. A lot of females between the ages of eighteen and forty, no doubt."

* * *

CORA STAYED HOME FROM SCHOOL. Quieter than normal and wrapped in Madeline's jumper, she tried to stay awake. She just couldn't face that dream again. Her mother took the boys to a play date at Caitlyn's. Right now, her Uncle Liam and Aunt Izzie were watching reruns of Game of Thrones and keeping an eye on her. Her Aunt Miren was next door, but she wasn't feeling well today either. Her uncle knocked on the half open door. "Still no sleep? Does your mother know you're staying awake on purpose?"

"Don't tell her. I just…can't face it. I need a break. I know I should be trying to get more sleep, but I'm just stuck."

"Your Aunt Miren just called. She's feeling better and is coming to relieve us. Please, darlin', ye need to let go and sleep. You're just making yourself sick. I've got a cup of valerian and chamomile tea, and I want you to drink it. It will help you relax."

Izzy came in then, crawling in next to Cora. "How about I stay a little while longer? Until you fall asleep?" Cora cuddled in next to her Aunt Izzy and was suddenly overcome with gratitude for her family.

* * *

Miren watched the headlights come into the driveway. Brigid was at her mother's house with the two smallest children. They were going to stay there until they figured out whether or not Cora was ill and contagious. Miren had a small window of time to speak with her nephew.

Finn came into the house and felt a hum of awareness before he even saw his aunt. He read her face plain as day. "Hello, Auntie. How's my girl?"

"She finally fell asleep. It's a fitful rest, though. I'm glad we have some time alone. We need to talk."

"I know." He'd known this was coming and resigned himself to it.

His aunt asked, "How much do you remember about that time before I left? When you were seeing that specialist?"

Miren's eyes were sad. "I know you were very young. Not much older than Colin, I think. Do you remember?"

"I was seven. I remember. I remember it all, Miren." Finn said. But that wasn't quite true. There were blank spots in his memory, likely due to his age and the stress of it all.

"You know your mother meant well by taking you to the specialist. Our mother wasn't a pleasant woman. I loved her, but there you have it. She said some pretty unkind things to me when I refused to hide my gifts. And she did, I suspect, treat you the same."

"She told me little boys who dealt in the devil's crafts would be kept out of Heaven." Finn said it flatly, like he was removed from the memory and talking about someone else. "And that I should turn from temptation."

"I'm sorry, Finn. But you know that's a bunch of bollocks. You were a good boy. What you experienced was a gift from God. Something to be used for good."

"Well, apparently my mother didn't think so. And at the time, I was afraid. Both because of what my grandmother said and because of what was happening to me. When mother took me to that specialist, I went willingly. I didn't want to be different. I felt like a freak. Then you and my mother fell out. It was after the headaches started. Now you're back and..."

"And you're getting bombarded from both sides, so to speak. Finn, you realize that by suppressing your psychic abilities, you changed your brain. And if Cora is right and we are...linked in some way, then you are having those headaches when we are most sensitive. When Cora's dreaming or I'm meditating. You've made yourself sick because of a bitter old woman's crusade to exorcise an imaginary demon. Cora feels alone in this. Ye never told Brigid or her what you could do when you were little. And now I'm part of that deception."

The voice came from behind them. Brigid said, "Never told me what?"

Finn's face blanched. He turned to her, smiling a false grin. Christ, he was in it now. "Hello, hen. The kids are all settled at their granny's?"

Brigid's eyes narrowed. "Finn, don't change the subject. What is it you never told me? Something about you as a child?"

Then from the other side of the room, a weak voice broke through. The three of them looked in the darkened doorway to see Cora. Her face was stricken. "That he's like me."

Brigid couldn't process. "What? Wait, back up a moment. Finn, what is going on? Miren?" Brigid looked like her head was about to pop off.

Finn looked like he was going to throw up. He scrubbed his face with his hands. "I didn't want you to find out like this. Either of you."

"What the bloody hell are you talking about, Finn? Maybe I'm a bit thickheaded. Cora said you were like her. In what way?" Finn almost recoiled at the tone. She was pissed, and she had every right to be. They both did.

"In the same way that Finn is like me. The dark ones who have the strongest McDubh blood," Miren said. "Finn was very young. His mother…"

"I'm sorry to interrupt, Miren, but I need for my husband to open his feckin' gob and tell me what's going on. Look at me, Finn. Look at me and tell me that you haven't been lying to me for our entire marriage. That you haven't been lying to your wife and daughter!"

"You don't understand, Brigid. When we met, it was in the past. My mother took me to this renowned psychiatrist. They were working wonders with hypnosis at this clinic in Cork. She…fixed it. Her words, not mine." He put his hands out flat in front of him.

"What do you mean, fixed it?"

"I was hypnotized when I was a small boy. Just like some people do to stop smoking. It suppressed my abilities. I was so young, and my grandmother was a bit of a fanatic."

"Finn, it doesn't matter what they did or said. It's bad enough that you never told me, but when Cora was born." Her voice caught. "You never said a word! Actually, that's not accurate. You said it wasn't from the Murphy side. That you didn't know where her abilities came from."

"I never said that. You assumed it. I told you it isn't from the Murphy side. It isn't. It's from another branch of the family completely. And I should have told you. But when you're told to keep a secret for so long, it becomes a part of you. Then it seemed too late. I'm so sorry."

"Apologize to your daughter," she spat out. "I'm not feeling particularly gracious right now. I'm sorry, Miren. I hate to have this out in front of you, but it appears you're the only one who has a clear head in the matter."

Finn watched tears well up in Cora's eyes. She'd been quiet for far too long. She croaked, "Would it have been so bad?" Finn's eyes stung with his own tears as she finished. "Would it have really been so bad to be like me?"

He went to her, getting down on his knees. He put his hands on her narrow shoulders. The betrayal in her eyes gutted him. "No, my darling. I would have been better off if I'd been as brave as you are. I always tried to be there for you. I always tried to help you through the visions. I just couldn't tell you. I was a coward."

"You didn't want to be a freak," she repeated his words. He shut his eyes for a moment, then he took her hand.

"I don't think I was a freak then. I don't think you are a freak now. But when you're five years old and you're scared out of your wits, and the adults are throwing around that ugly word, it makes an impression. My grandmother wore my mother down. It drove Miren away because…"

Miren interjected. "Because he suffered terrible headaches afterward, and they wouldn't undo it. They wouldn't even try." She watched as Finn recoiled at the words. "Oh my God, lad. You didn't know. You didn't know that you could undo it, did you?"

"What are you saying, Miren? I don't see how it can be undone."

"Hypnosis only works if the person is willing. You chose to suppress your gifts, to put some sort of lock on it. I don't know what all happened when you finally went through with it, but if you can lock down that part of your mind, you can unlock it."

"I can't just decide. Some shrink put me under. Then it was weeks of therapy." But Miren's words made sense and he was stunned by the possibility.

Brigid came in the room and asked, "What kind of therapy, Finn? Like psychotherapy?"

"I don't remember. I just remember my mother taking me in every week." He started rubbing his neck. "They wouldn't let her come in with me."

Miren gave him a pitying look. "I'm sorry, my dear. I didn't know about the rest of it. But I have people you can talk to about this. They are familiar with the clinic in Cork where your mother took you. Apparently, it's been shut down. I think they could help you, Finn."

He looked at Cora and realized that what he did and said in this moment was very important. Like the adults in his boyhood, it would make an impression on her and mold her. "I think I'd like that information. If you are telling me that I can reverse this. That I can become…the way I was before, then I'll do it." Something seemed to shift in Cora's body. He felt it. Not forgiveness, maybe, but relief. And he felt like a horrible bastard for not trusting his women with this secret.

* * *

FINN WATCHED his wife from across the room. "Brigid, please. Just stop. You stay put. I'll be the one to leave. If it's really what you want, then I will sleep in the boys' room." He stood there, unable to comprehend how his life had taken such a wrong turn with a few overheard words. He deserved this. "I should have told you. I was afraid you'd run for the hills."

She gave him a hard look. "Yes, you should have. You didn't trust me, Finn. After everything we've been to each other, you didn't trust me with this."

"I didn't tell you at first because it was so long in the past. The headaches had stopped. It was a part of my life I wanted to forget. It's a blur really. I didn't want to scare you off. I loved you so much, Brigid. And I couldn't take the chance you'd think I was some nutter who was delusional. I made a mistake. Then Cora's gifts emerged, and I was ashamed. She was such a brave lass. A wonder. And how could I tell her that I'd agreed to such a thing?"

She turned her back on him. "Either you are going or I am. I can't share a bed with a man who so easily deceived me."

He left with his pillow and a spare blanket. He passed Cora's room, and the light was out. "Da," she said softly.

He leaned in her doorway. "Yes, love?"

"I forgive you. You were a child, and what they did to you was wrong. I forgive you for not telling me."

He exhaled, and his voice was tight and hoarse with emotion. "Thank you, my sweet lass."

"I heard what you said to Mam. You didn't want me to follow down the same path. To try to hide who I was. You wanted me to be braver than you were. But you were young, Da. And you didn't have the same support I do. You didn't have the O'Briens." Finn hiccupped on a sob, holding it in. The O'Briens were what had made the difference. Brigid had made the difference. *She wore your mother down.* Brigid would have never even considered taking Cora to that clinic. Cora continued, as if to twist the knife. "But Da, you really hurt Mam. You're really in the doghouse."

"I know, and she has the right to be angry. So do you, my heart."

"I've been staying awake, hiding from those dreams. Do you think maybe you could sleep with me instead of the boys' room? I normally lean in favor of female solidarity, when one of you men has stepped in it, but you are my daddy. That trumps everything."

Stepped in it...Female solidarity. This kid is too much, he thought. "You are so smart; it scares me sometimes. I am truly glad you're on my side."

Cora could hear the smile. That was good. She didn't want him to be sad. "Come on, Da. I need my wingman. Maybe if ye get your superpowers back, we'll get on Oprah." Finn cracked off a laugh. This kid was too much.

* * *

COLTON INSTITUTE
Rathdrum, Co. Wicklow

Finn sat across from Dr. Saoirse McNamara, assessing her. She wasn't what he'd expected. She had cropped salt-and-pepper hair, intelligent eyes, and a lot of degrees from great schools. "Miren has told me a bit about you and your daughter. I've never seen such a clear example of psychic ability being genetic. I can help you, Mr. Murphy. But I'm going to be up front with you about my desire to study the three generations. Your aunt, yourself, and your daughter. It's remarkable, and I think we can learn a lot from each other."

Finn lifted his chin. "I can't promise that. My daughter is ten years old. She still plays with dolls. I don't want her studied like a zoo animal. Is your help dependent on that?"

"Of course not. We'll address it at another time," she said smoothly. Like a woman who had the patience to wait for the big game.

Miren came to his defense. "Why don't we talk about what exactly the clinic in Cork was up to twenty-eight years ago?"

"It's simple. From what we know about that particular clinic, they were combining hypnosis with aversion therapy. It certainly explains the headaches. Sometimes they used electrical shock, sometimes they'd administer a drug to induce a headache. In younger children, it was often something as simple as high dose caffeine tablets melted on the tongue. They reinforce over and over again that trying to access your abilities will lead to discomfort."

Finn wasn't sold. "I don't understand how they could convince me to get a headache."

"Have you heard of Dr. Pavlov?"

"Yes, the dogs. So, you're saying they trained a response."

"It's a theory. I believe they thought this absurd treatment was actually working. They thought they'd programmed your body to revolt and set off pain receptors if you used your gift, causing the headaches. I'm afraid my opinion is a little less dazzling, but also less self-serving. I think you are actually taxing your brain with that box you've kept locked."

"Box?"

"I've seen other patients from that clinic. Some came to me just to take part in the studies we do. The thing about hypnosis is the person has to be willing. They have to believe it's possible and submit, so to speak, or the hypnosis doesn't work. It's not like the movies. It's a deeply relaxed state where your mind is vulnerable to suggestion. Some of them were older, less cooperative. They remember, you see. They never really went under. During the session, they were told to envision a box. They were to imagine themselves putting all of the scary dreams, the visions, the intuitions, and anything else atypical of the *normal* human brain and lock it away in a box. One young man envisioned a large padlock. Another saw chains around the box. Sometimes the box was big, other times small enough to put in your hand. But the details didn't matter. They were to lock it away and not open the box."

"Which means it can be opened. You don't tell someone not to do something unless it can be done," Finn said. He looked at Miren and asked, "Did my mother know?"

"I don't know. You'll need to ask her, my dear. From the sounds of it, she wasn't present for the treatments. They may not have told her what they were doing. I think she would have put a stop to it if she knew how far it went."

"There's no way in hell I would leave my child with strangers and have no idea what they were doing." Finn's voice was bitter.

"That can't be undone, but the question you have to ask yourself is what do you want. This unlocking of the box isn't complicated, you see. But everyone is different, and you may get overwhelmed when it all comes back. Both memories of what they did in those sessions, and the return of your abilities. According to your aunt, you would have a strong sense of smell during the visions. Smell things others couldn't. How did the information come to you?"

"In dreams, like Cora."

"She's young. I suspect that as she ages, she'll be able to do as Miren does. She'll be able to bring forth the information with deep meditation. Honestly, there may be more to both of you than you realize. I have one client who does things through touch. Are you sure?

"I am. I have to do this for my daughter as much as for myself." *And I have to try to save my marriage.*

* * *

3 HOURS EARLIER...

"What in the bloody hell do you mean you didn't go with him!" Sorcha Mullen rarely raised her voice at her children, especially in front of their own kids. But this child was going to be the death of her. "Brigid Murphy, what could you be thinking?"

"He lied to me, Mam! He kept it from me for almost twelve years! No, I didn't go with him! I haven't spoken two words to him since I threw him out of our bedroom!"

"Jesus, child. You really do get my temper rolling." She looked at her daughter and it was like a mirror. She'd certainly given Sean a run for his money in their younger years. She said, "He was afraid. And not much scares Finn. I'd imagine once Cora's gifts emerged, he felt it was too late to come clean."

Brigid raised her voice, defending her position. "That's what he said. It's no excuse!" Sorcha started laughing. "What is so funny! Nothing about this is remotely funny!"

Her father walked in at that moment, raised his brows and flipped around to make a run for it. "Sean, my love. The day has arrived!"

Defeated, he turned to face her. "And which day is that, hen?"

"Remember how we marveled that Brigid and Finn came together so easily. That there hadn't been even one bump in the road? After all of the blood, sweat, and tears her brothers have suffered, and you and I, that this little peahen got off easy because she was a lass?"

Brigid's fists were on her hips, and Sean thought she looked so much like her mother in a temper, he felt the insane urge to giggle. "Well, then. So it seems. Do I want to know, or can I grab that bag of crisps and go watch the match?"

"I'll tell you everything later, sweetheart. Carry on."

Brigid glared at him as he grabbed the crisps and left in a hurry. Then she burst into tears. Her mother came around the counter and took her in her arms as she fell apart in racking sobs. "It's okay, my sweet girl. This can be mended. And what's more, it is worth mending. It's everything. Your love and the family you've made with Finn are everything. When I am in my grave and gone to the hereafter, my legacy and your father's will be that we taught our children the value of love. That O'Briens mate for life like seagulls."

"Cranes, mother. It's cranes that mate for life."

Cora finally piped in with, "And puffins! And Macaws!"

Sorcha waved a hand in dismissal, "You get my point. Now, you take that oldest child of yours and start driving to Wicklow. Finn should not be facing his early childhood trauma without his wife. And Cora is a part of this. Go, and hold his hand while he faces down these demons."

"Maybe I should leave Cora. Just until Finn and I are on speaking terms. We may have traumatized her last night."

Sorcha said, "That child is tougher than all of us."

Cora marveled that they were talking like she wasn't in the room. "She's got that right. I let Da sleep with me last night. Forgave him within minutes. It's you, Mam, who's the stubborn little harpy."

Brigid's jaw was on the floor. *Stubborn little harpy?* Then she and her mother burst into laughter until there were tears coming down their faces.

* * *

FINN PULLED off his jumper and untucked his t-shirt. It was hot in the room. His heart was racing. He hated this. He felt trapped. The doctor watched him, waiting. "You are very stressed, Mr. Murphy. I need you to try to clear your mind. The more you can relax the better. I'd imagine this is bringing some suppressed memories to the surface." He wished his wife was with him. He needed to see her face. He felt a tingling of awareness as if he'd summoned the little she-devil from her lair.

That's when he heard it. It was unmistakable. "I want to see my husband. If you don't go get him, I'm comin' through that door." *Brigid. She came.*

He was out the door and down the hall in a flash. He flew by Miren, who was in another room. She was doing some sort of deep breathing with another person from the research team. She opened her eyes and stood, coming behind him. He saw Brigid over the intake counter and was through the door and in her arms in a flash. "I'm so sorry. Oh, God. Please, love. Forgive me." Then he saw Cora and pulled her close as well. "My beautiful girls. Please, forgive me."

"I love you, ye thick headed lout! Don't you know that? And although you'll have to make it up to me, I do forgive you. You can start by getting me past Nurse Ratched."

The male nurse at the counter gave a crooked smile, just happy to be out of the line of fire.

* * *

CORA SAT with her Aunt Miren, down the hall from her father. Her mother was in the next room, watching through the glass. "It's okay if it doesn't work, Cora dear. It just

61

occurred to me to try. You said you were stuck. That the visions in your dreams have yet to take shape. I know we're different, but maybe together we can bring this thing into focus. I want to show you what they taught me here."

"I'm afraid. A lot of my visions show..." She looked at the glass. "Death. Or the dead. It's not always clear. Sometimes it's like a puzzle. Sometimes, like with my Uncle William, they come to me to give a message. I'm afraid. This has something to do with water. I'm so scared something's going to happen to Uncle Michael or Josh. If I see one of them..." She was shaking now.

"Anytime you want to stop, we will. But just think, Cora. You could help. The future is not set. Remember what you did for Alanna and Aidan, and then again for your Uncle Liam and Izzy? You are a wonder, my dear girl, and I'm here with you. Let me help you and perhaps some good will come from it. "

* * *

FINN'S BREATH was slow and steady. The metronome ticked and he felt his heart rate go down. He wanted this. He really did. After the four of them had a sit-down with Dr. McNamara, he took strength from his family. If Cora could face this every night, he could do no less. He felt and heard the things around him, and then he drifted away.

He heard the doctor, although he was in a dark room with no furniture and no windows. He could see nothing but a small box. It looked so harmless. He lifted it from the floor and was amused to see the bike lock from his first bicycle. He remembered the combination. It was the year his dog was born. 1989. He opened it, and then he looked up. He was in a similar room to the one he left. But the doctors were different. One pinched-faced man in particular sent a spike of fear through him.

Your mother can't hear you, so you may as well settle. This is what she agreed to. Now hold still. Sensors were hooked to his fingers. Then the shocks came. Not enough to do any lasting damage, but just enough to hurt. The first burst of pain brought him out of it.

Finn opened his eyes, wiping the tears away. The tears of a small, terrified boy. He'd do his best to heal that boy and put him to bed. And to make sure Cora never felt as desperate as he'd felt in that room. "I remember," he said. He wasn't sure if he felt different, so to speak. He just felt lighter. He felt a hum of light thrum softly through his body, starting with his temples and down to his toes. He felt normal. His normal and no one else's.

CORA FELT the moment her Aunt Miren joined her. She was so cold. The water was pulling her. "Calm yourself, lass. Try to see past the panic. This isn't happening to you. Try to focus your eyes."

The saltwater burned, but she saw the grey sky. She saw the chopping waves. "Can you go back, my dear? Can you reverse it like a movie?"

She couldn't do that. All she could do was feel and fight the pull of the current. "What else do you feel. Think about your feet and work your way up. Is anything else happening?" She did, and it wasn't until she reached her arms that she felt anything but cold water. Good God. Someone was holding her. Someone was trying to keep ahold on her. But the water was so cold. The swells tossed them around. "Very good, Cora. Who is it? Can you look?"

Another wave crested overhead, and her eyes stung. Her

lungs were heavy and her mouth was saturated with saltwater. She felt the tug-of-war between someone else who was struggling to keep hold and the angry pulls of the sea. Then she saw it. The bow of a ship, other people in the water, and finally looking toward the arm that tethered her to another. A familiar face looked back at her. Cora gasped and bolted to her feet. "Oh, God. Maddie."

CHAPTER 7

GALWAY FERRY DOCK, CO. GALWAY

*J*osh had a bad feeling as he left the car park to head for home. It was too windy to be out on the bike, but Seany had the car so he could bring back the microwave. The ferries were headed back, and the weather was turning. It had been a sunny, nice morning. But the tropical storms and hurricanes off the coast of the U.S. were causing havoc on the entire Atlantic. The forecast was good for today, so this storm had come out of nowhere. It made him wonder if there really was a Poseidon and if someone had angered him. The line he worked for already had all of their boats in, but there were a few still on Inishmore that had to get the day-tourists home. He decided the best place for him was the cottage, because the RNLI had a small boat station just ten minutes from his home. If he was going to get called in, better to be close and ready. That's when Cora's words came back to him. *I don't know, but you will. All I know is you should be ready.*

* * *

MADELINE WAS EXHAUSTED. Inishmore was a big island. And although they were shuttled to various sites, they'd still done a lot of walking. They'd cut off early when their driver was rung by the ferry captain. They were headed back early due to incoming storms. She saw it, of course. The squall line was impressive. Now they were on the boat, and she read the tension in the Captain's eyes. His skipper bit out, "I told you we shouldn't have gone without the navigation working. We're blind in this!"

"Shut your gob. I know exactly where I am. How do you think we got around before all of these gadgets!" Normally Madeline would agree. She'd banned technology during the tour lectures. The groans at her no phone rule were loud. Photos would be taken for five minutes, then phones were put away. They ended up rather enjoying themselves. And they talked. They actually talked to each other. The ages varied from seventy to ten years old. She looked over at the small boy. He was as beautiful as he was silent. As if he sensed it, he turned and met her eyes. She smiled, then curled into her jacket as someone moved to go inside, leaving her to be assaulted by sea mist and wind. She stayed, though. Sea sickness only got worse if you were in the cabin. That squall line was getting closer. She tried not to think about it. She heard the captain's radio squawking. "He's telling us to turn around. The storm is hitting the coast from the north!"

"I'll never get my bearings if we turn around. Just keep your wits about you and keep your eyes open. I need to come south of that bigger boat that left ahead of us."

Maddie was getting scared. She looked again at the small Welsh family with the young son. His mother had told her that the boy hadn't spoken a word since he was five. He'd been witness to a bus accident in Cardiff. One minute he was holding her hand, then he jerked her back with more strength than a boy of five should have. Right where she'd been about to walk, a van ran over the cross walk, blowing the red light, and crashing into a public bus. Rhys had gone somewhere, according to the mother. He'd withdrawn from the world, even though he functioned in it.

Right now, the boy looked worried. He was fighting with his mother in their own nonverbal tug of war. He wanted her to put on the life preserver under the seat. He struggled with one of his own, starting to cause a scene. It was hopelessly big. Maddie looked underneath her seat to find a perfectly new children's life preserver. She struggled to walk, lurching with the rocking of the boat. She knelt down and handed it to him. The mother smiled, "No doubt it will make him feel better." She shrugged and slipped one over her head.

Then Madeline fastened the boy's. She kissed him on the top of the head. "It'll all be grand. Just a bit of Irish weather. The sea is temperamental in the autumn. Don't worry yourself, Rhys." She stood to return to her seat when a wave crashed over the side of the boat so hard it knocked her off her feet. She felt the pain as her shoulder made contact with something on the boat deck. The bow went upward and people started to scream as the inevitable crash downward on the water was coming. But it was so much worse than they could have imagined as metal hit metal.

MADELINE WAS FLOATING. There was no sound, just the chilling silence of the sea. She looked up, but she couldn't get her bearings. She rolled and rocked. *Watch the bubbles.* She heard her father's voice plain as day. Those easy summer days when he'd taught them all to swim.

The bubbles went above her head, and she saw light. The sky was grey, but it was still full daylight out. She pumped her legs, which only made her lungs burn more. She saw someone above her. She broke the surface, surrounded by total chaos, and a pair of arms came around her. It was Rhys. "Oh, God. You've got your jacket on!" She looked around for his parents, but the swells were so big. People were screaming as the boat surged, half sunken. They had to get away from it. That's when she saw the orange ring. Like the hand of God passing it to her. The ring would be their salvation, unless they froze to death. The water was stabbing cold. She swam, tugging him away from the sinking ship. They'd get sucked under if they were too close. She reached the ring and actually screamed a little at the victory. She put it over the boy's head, and he shook his head fiercely. "Yes, my lad. I'll drag you under, otherwise. That jacket won't hold us both. I've got the rope and I won't let go. Just keep breathing and keep your legs moving."

They were helpless against the pull of the sea. Tossed like rag dolls, but with enough will to cling to each other. They were caught in some sort of current that pulled them out of the path of the rolling boat, and she prayed to God it wouldn't pull them any farther away from the shore. She couldn't see land. Oh, God. She couldn't see anything but water and sky.

Josh's phone rang, but it wasn't his Lifeboat mobile. It was his personal one. "Cora?"

She was hysterical. "Josh! It's Maddie. Oh, God! She's in the water. I think it's one of the ferries! Josh, you have to call the lifeboat! I can't get hold of Michael. He's in the air!" But no sooner had she said it than the other phone went off.

"Hold on, Cora. Don't hang up!" He answered it. Two ferries collided between Inishmore and Galway. One sank, one taking water. *Jesus Christ.* He had one of the men in the area driving by to get him. It's the system they'd worked out in case he didn't have the car. They'd sent a message out for all hands to be ready as soon as the storm started brewing. Everyone who hadn't been consuming alcohol within the last 12 hours was to be ready for duty.

He grabbed his gear and kept Cora on speaker. Cora said, "She's with someone else. I don't know who. But the arm looked like a child. She was trying to keep her head above water. She was trying to keep them together. She's so cold, Josh! Oh my God! I should have seen it sooner!"

"Cora, calm down honey. Please. You are more help than you know. Did you see anything else?" When she said that she hadn't, he promised he'd call her as soon as he could. Then he jumped in his fellow volunteer's car and they were headed toward the Furbogh dock. His heart was thumping in his chest. He dialed Mary. "Mary, I need to know where Madeline is right now? I swear I have a reason for asking."

Mary didn't seem to think it was an odd question at all. "She's in Inishmore leading a tour group for her thesis. She called me from the ferry dock. Do you need her number?"

* * *

CORA WAS CALMER NOW. The sight of Maddie in that water had undone her. She remembered all too vividly the dream she'd had about Eve, that had ended so tragically. Was Maddie going to die? She said, "This dream was different. This whole thing is different. It's like I'm a participant. Like I was in the water with Maddie. Why is it different?"

Miren was not sure herself. She looked at the nurse and Brigid for guidance but got none. "You told me you've seen those who have passed on. That they were messengers. But you never looked through their eyes. You're right. This is different. It's no coincidence. You are seeing through the eyes of another person for a reason. Someone who is with this young woman you know."

Cora wiped the tears from her eyes, but they just kept coming. She hoped to God she wasn't too late.

MICHAEL O'BRIEN'S heart sank as he took in the scene below him. The huge swells had come up so quickly, these people didn't know what hit them. According to the captain of the second boat, he'd heeded the Coast Guard warning to turn around and head back to the island. Apparently, the primary boat had not. The why of it? He had no idea. The collision had been catastrophic for the shore-bound boat. They weren't even sure if everyone got out of the interior cabin.

Michael saw the larger of the Coast Guard boats keeping its distance. They didn't have great visibility and they didn't want to run over anyone or hit ship debris. The co-pilot guided them in while the pilot was getting in position to drop Michael and his partner into the area where they saw the group of people huddled together in the water. Some of them had life jackets, some didn't, but they were holding their own. He selfishly thanked God this hadn't been a boat out of Doolin. Those ferry lines didn't run this long into the autumn. He'd called on his way to the site to make sure Katie hadn't been on one of the boats. She spent a lot of time on Inisheer, but the two boats had been coming from Inishmore.

He checked his buddy's suit and tank, and his buddy did the same for him. Then it was time to roll.

THE THIRD TIME Madeline's head went under, and the line

went taut, the little boy slid the ring over her coughing, exhausted figure. "Okay, you're right. Just don't let go, okay. Get closer. I'll keep you warm." But she said it through blue lips. She was scared. Terrified, actually. Because she couldn't hear anyone anymore. She thought she'd heard a helicopter, but it was far off in the distance.

The current had pulled them out of the kill zone from the sinking boat, but then they'd kept going. She looked at Rhys. His lips were blue. He could barely hang on to the rope. "Come here, love." She pulled him as close as she could get him and brought his hand to her mouth. She placed a kiss on his white knuckles. "We're going to be okay." She saw his tears and knew they weren't for himself. She hadn't had any family on that boat, but he had. He was so small he'd been thrown out of the boat not far from where she'd landed. Her lip was bleeding, but she was hoping the weather would keep the sharks away. She'd bitten her lip and hit her shoulder when the boat had lurched her forward and across the deck. She should never have gotten up. Then again, if she hadn't, Rhys wouldn't have a life jacket on right now.

She said soothing words to him and prayed. Those Coast Guard helicopters would spot the boat wreckage first. Would they keep looking? What about the Royal Lifeboat? Ireland might be small, but they had plenty of men and women who volunteered for both. That made her think of Josh. Would he be called out? He didn't know she was on one of the boats, but he was the type of man who would help if he could. She didn't want to die. She wanted to see her nieces and nephew grow up. She wanted her own children. She wanted to see her little sister again. If she lived through this, she wouldn't waste a single minute.

Their body temperatures kept dropping. It had to be worse for him. He was slightly built. She looked at the sky and saw the squall line overhead. It had been to the northwest, she thought. That was good, right? Maybe they were near land. That's when the rain started like someone had turned the shower on over their heads. A downpour that just made the sea angrier. "Hang on, little man. Please!" She felt the pull of the sea trying to separate them. "No! Rhys, you have to hang on!" But they were both so cold. Their fingers wouldn't work, and their skin was slippery. His eyes were panicked as he looked behind her. She knew. She felt the suction. Then they were both tossed up and she felt him ripped from her arms. A wall of water crashed overhead, and it took every ounce of her energy to stay in the safety of the life preserver. It plunged her downward, scrambling her in the moving water until she thought her lungs would burst and her arms would break. When she surfaced, she barely had ahold on the ring. She couldn't see anything. The rain pelted her face. "Rhys! Rhys!" But he couldn't answer her even if he heard her. He was just gone.

* * *

Josh picked up their first person about a quarter mile from the wreck site. His heart was in overdrive. Cora had known something was going to happen. And she'd known in her own way, that he would end up here. That had to be for a reason. There was a nasty current which pulled these people toward the northwest. There could be more. Cora said she'd felt like she was being pulled by a current, and Madeline had been with someone. A child maybe. "Do you have the Coast Guard online?"

"Yes, I've got a Doolin dispatcher as a go between."

"Tell her to ask the passengers they've pulled out of the water if there's a kid missing? A kid and a young blonde woman."

It took about ten excruciating minutes. "Affirmative. A

ten-year-old got thrown clear before his parents hit the water. Rhys Llewelyn. The tour group is missing their guide as well. A young blonde woman named…"

"Madeline Nagle," Josh finished and the man looked at him like he was Lazarus back from the dead. Josh whispered, "I will find you, Madeline. I swear it. I will not leave this water until I find you." He turned to the boat captain. "Head northwest. That current washed one person down the coast, there could be more. The Coast Guard has the crash site covered."

"You know her, don't you?" The man's face was grave. The other men in the boat were quiet. They spoke English out of courtesy instead of the Irish so engrained in the people of the west coast. He'd heard the Gaelic fly between different members of the unit, but they were polite enough to include him in English when he was part of the group. He answered the man, his voice rough with emotion.

"Yes, I know her." *And I love her. She's not mine, but I love her.*

* * *

MADELINE SOBBED until her body was limp. She was so cold and tired, but that wasn't the worst of it. She'd lost him. That little boy whose mother and father would never be the same if he drowned. She just hadn't been strong enough to hold on. She'd failed him. But it didn't mean he was dead. She had to get her shit together. If she could get to shore she could help them trace where the current had taken him. She needed a miracle.

She couldn't feel her fingers anymore. And she knew if she fell asleep, she was dead. She was settling into the hypothermia like the beginning of a long sleep. She'd worn a down vest and cashmere sweater. It wasn't heavy, but it had some thermal properties. She didn't know if she was still wearing her slip-on shoes. Her feet were so numb she couldn't tell. She shook with the effort of keeping her body temperature from going in the basement, but she was losing the fight. The saltwater saturated her eyes, nose, and throat. When she coughed, there was salty fluid being expelled from her lungs. She was so thirsty. Surrounded by water with nothing to drink. She wanted to sleep. She wanted her mother. She wanted to see Rhys floating in front of her, alive and fighting.

The temptation to close her eyes was strong. She was being pelted with rain, and the sea water made them burn. She almost missed the search light. She saw it, then she didn't. She wondered if it had been a mirage, but then she saw it again. Her heart rate spiked. "Here!" Her throat was raw. "Here!"

Josh saw the figure in the water for a split second, then it disappeared. The wind whipped against his face as he strained in the grey light to see her. It was a frustration to be in the time between full darkness and light. The weather being what it was, he was left with little natural light to see by, and everything took on a monochromatic hue. It left the landscape a vast stretch of blue and grey. But he had seen something. A flash of orange that could be a life preserver. "Slow down, I saw something!" he yelled to the captain. With the next swell, it came into focus. A cascade of wet hair and an orange ring . He was in the water before he thought better of it. He pumped his arms and legs, his rescue can bobbing behind him. Then he saw her face. Fear and relief pounded through him as he closed the distance. "Madeline!"

He grabbed her just as a swell overtook him. She said, "Don't let me go! Oh, please. Don't let me go." She was so weak she couldn't help him. The water crested over both of them and Madeline choked on the sea water. She clung to him, weeping and coughing.

"I won't let go, honey. Never," he said.

"I lost him. The boy who was with me! I lost him!" She was hysterical, but she was too weak to do anything but cooperate and let him hold her. He towed her against his chest as the lifeboat got closer. He threw the line to his mates, then let them tow them both in. He handed Madeline up and then accepted assistance. "We need to get these two medical treatment," he said, as he pulled more hot pads and blankets from the storage area. The first passenger rescued passenger was huddled under the thermal blankets. He was uninjured and his color was returning.

The man on communications duty said, "There will be an ambulance waiting at the Furbogh dock. The other lifeboat is headed into Galway with two more passengers that got separated from the group. The Coast Guard has the rest. The crew and passengers are all accounted for but one."

"Rhys," Madeline croaked. Then she finally looked into the face of her rescuer. She was curled up in his arms, wrapped in blankets and a hot pad in an attempt to get her body temperature back up. She couldn't process what she was seeing. "Josh? Am I dreaming?"

"I wish you were, sweetheart. Just close your eyes, Madeline." But she didn't. She touched his face.

"Thank you, Josh. I don't know how you found me but thank you."

"I'll explain later. Just rest." He pulled her against him and kissed her head. "Just rest, my angel."

She exhaled, closing her eyes. Then she was asleep.

Josh panicked, "Is she going into shock? Should we keep her awake?"

But the medic was already on it. "Her pulse is sluggish but she's okay. She's exhausted, lad. Just keep her warm." Then the man put a blanket over him as well. His wetsuit was good, but he'd still gone into the drink. "That's a good lad. This is quite a first run, and ye did well."

Josh felt Madeline's body start to warm, and he shuddered with relief. He would let her take it all, until he was an ice cube, if he could. If only he'd been here sooner, he could have found them both together. If that little boy was dead, she was never going to forgive herself. No one could have done more, he had no doubt, but she still wouldn't forgive herself.

* * *

UNIVERSITY HOSPITAL GALWAY

Caitlyn ran into her friend's arms as he enveloped her into a big bear hug. "Seamus! I'm so glad you're here. They won't tell us anything."

Seamus said, "They're overwhelmed, love. Too many patients at once. They've farmed out the worst of the injured to Dublin and Cork. If they didn't fly her out, that's a good sign." He slapped a hand in Patrick's palm. "Izzy's tied up in surgery. I did get hold of germ boy, however. He's on his way."

Seamus looked over at who must be Caitlyn's parents and other sister. The mother was as lovely as the daughters. It was the father's expression that hit him right in the gut, though. He put himself in this man's shoes on just about every level. Daughters were their kryptonite. They had no defense against them.

Caitlyn's phone rang as Seamus went back into the bowels of the emergency room, looking for answers. "Seany, have you heard from Josh or Michael? We can't get hold of them. She'll want to know about her tour group and the boy.

Oh, God. Those poor parents!" She started sobbing and Patrick took the phone.

Patrick said, "Just stay safe, brother. We can't take another tragedy right now."

Patrick rang off and walked over to the seating area where Caitlyn was crying it out with her mother and sister. He handed her the phone just as Charlie walked in. Her eyes were wild, looking around the room. "Where's my brother?"

"He's back out there. He said he wasn't coming in until they found that boy," Patrick said. Charlie's breathing started speeding up. She had her hand on her belly. Patrick said, "Christ, you're not in labor, surely?"

She snapped, "No! It's a protective instinct. I'm not having this baby for three more weeks!"

Patrick backed up as he said, "Darlin, aren't you thirty-nine weeks along?"

"My mother didn't have both of us until forty-two weeks. I'm not going to have this baby this week or next. I'm going to have it in three weeks!" She snarled at him.

"Tadgh, she's scaring me." Patrick took another step back.

Tadgh shrugged and said, "It's called she-bear syndrome or something like that. Instead of nesting, she's bearing."

Charlie rounded on him, pointing in his face. "Call me a bear one more time." She paused between each word, as if to make sure he didn't miss the threat.

The devil just winked at her. "You know I love when you get tough with me, love. Now, there's a vending machine right over there. If you don't bite Patrick, I'll get you some crisps."

She cocked her head. "Salt and vinegar?"

"If they don't have salt and vinegar, I'll take you downstairs for a burger."

She looked back over her shoulder at Patrick, as if trying to weigh kicking his ass or getting bribed with food. "Deal."

Patrick looked at his in-laws and wife. They had their jaws collectively dropped. "I'm going to go call Mam. They'll want an update, and I want to check on the kids."

He started to leave when Seamus reemerged. Seamus said, "She's stable. The thermal blanket is helping stabilize her body temperature. She's just come out of x-ray. She's got a scapula fracture and had to have three stitches below her lower lip. Bottom line, she's being admitted. They need to watch her and follow up with an orthopedic specialist about the shoulder. The good news is that she's going to be okay. She's exhausted and they've given her some pain meds. She's going to need it as the feeling starts coming back into her feet and hands. Things may get rather uncomfortable. Given what she's been through, she's very lucky. I got them to agree to two people at a time to sit with her. Perhaps her parents to start?"

Ronan and Bernadette jumped up and were through the door in an instant. Charlie waddled over to hug Caitlyn and Mary and hoped to God her brother was safe. People always talked about sibling rivalry, but they never talked about sibling love. A love that could be so deep and nurturing that the thought of losing them could bring you to your knees. The time she'd been separated from her brother was even more difficult than the beatings her father had dished out to her with regularity. She'd felt the loss of him like an amputation. She'd had her reasons for leaving, but the physical separation from Josh had been a deep and wide cavern of pain and anxiety that, at times, seemed uncrossable. She just really, really wanted to talk to her brother right now.

* * *

JOSH WAS STARVING. The nutrition drink they'd forced down his throat at the dock was doing very little. He just couldn't go back and tell Madeline they hadn't found that little boy. He couldn't do it. The kid had a life jacket on. That was the good news. But it had been at least a couple of hours since he'd first hit the water. It was getting dark now, but there was hope. The rain was down to a drizzle and the wind wasn't so fierce. He didn't want to think about going home to his warm bed while there was a little boy out on the open sea. The realization that the child couldn't scream for help just made the situation worse. He didn't want to call Cora again. It was too much to put on her. She couldn't control how it all came to her and she needed to rest. They were home from Wicklow now, and no doubt she'd have called if she knew anything more. She'd helped him find Madeline, and for that alone he'd owe the girl until he was an old man.

It was only when Cora heard that Madeline was safe and in the hospital that she finally fell asleep. Miren had retired as well, strangely depleted. She hadn't told them about her session with Cora. Not the whole of it. She didn't understand it herself. Brigid tucked Declan and Colin in and kissed them. Then she went to break the awkward silence that had cropped up between her and her husband. He stood at the bedroom window, looking out into the rainy night. She came in and shut the door, not knowing whether to hug him or interrogate him. And that was a first.

Her mother was right. Things were so easy for them. The main reason for that, if she was being honest, was that Finn always knew how to handle her. He knew just when to push her and just when to sit back and let her tire herself out. He'd always been what she needed. And the first sign of trouble, she'd thrown him out of their bed. "You shouldn't have lied to me, Finn."

His head hung off his shoulders. He was in low slung jeans and shirtless. So beautiful he was hard to look at sometimes. His hair was out of the tie, spilling over his shoulders in glossy black waves. His skin was so smooth, she wanted to taste it. How had they gotten here?

Finn answered tightly, "I know, Brigid. And I've said I'm sorry every way I can. Now, if you want me to sleep elsewhere, I will. I can't do this with you right now."

She bristled. She'd almost given a counter apology, but it died on her tongue. "Finn. I fail to see how you can justify getting pissy with me right now."

He rounded on her. "You wouldn't see!" The memories that had washed over him in the clinic were disjointed, but the fear and pain were fresh. As if it happening in the present. They'd let him start to drift off. Ask him if he smelled anything. Would wait until his abilities would start to surface, then they'd give him a dose of something in his IV and the headache would start. He had a flash of a little girl seizing in the room next to his. He'd heard the commotion and gone over to see her. Yelled for help. They'd ordered him back to bed. In time He'd tell Brigid everything, but not today. "I can't even put it into words," he croaked. "You have no idea the fucking ringer I just got put through!"

She stopped the caustic comment and closed her mouth. He was right. She hadn't even asked him. She was so used to him being okay. Being the steady, strong one. The cool breeze to her fire. Guilt washed over her. "Finn, Cora was so upset. Everything happened so fast. Then we were in separate cars. But I should have asked. I should have made the time to stop and talk to you." She teared up, wanting to fix everything and hating that she couldn't. "I hate this. I don't want distance between us."

He sighed, knowing that this wasn't really her fault. None of it was. "I understand. You're right. I don't know what I'm saying. I'm just a little raw right now." He turned back around, looking out the window again.

Brigid didn't have it in her to stay angry with him. His body trembled when she touched his back. Then she was in his arms. He crushed her to him, his mouth hard on hers. He had her pressed to the wall and practically tore her pants off. "I need in you." His words were husky and edgy as he freed himself from his jeans. He palmed her sex with one hand as he filled his other hand with her auburn hair. He took her mouth, deep and thorough.

Finn knew sex wasn't going to solve all their problems, but right now he needed this from her. That stain of a memory from his childhood self needed to take a back seat. He needed to remember who he was now. He was thirty-five years old, a father, a husband, a lover. He slowed down as he sheathed himself inside her. She moaned his name and he pushed her hair off her face. "Look at me. I want to see your face." He needed her to ground him to the present.

Her green eyes met his dark ones and suddenly nothing else mattered. He slid her top off and took her mouth more gently. He needed this connection. He crooned to her in Gaelic, lovers' words, flexing his hips as he filled her. He palmed her ass, her legs tight around his waist, and set a pace that was sure to send her through the roof. He felt just when she let go, going deep as a scream ripped from her throat and her core fisted his cock.

He let her ride it out, reveling in the way she whimpered as she came. She was singly the biggest pain in his ass. But she was also the breath and blood of his body. She was everything. And she was his. With that thought, she was flung onto the bed. "Get on your hands and knees. I want to fill you up." She obeyed, displaying her ass and spread legs. She moaned his name as he parted her flesh and slid deep. He held her hips as he started a punishing pace. She arched as she took all of him, her smooth white skin against his darker hips. Her glossy waves of auburn hair over her face as she came again. He bundled her hair in his fist as he looked up into their bedroom mirror. When he saw her dazed face, pink cheeks, glassy eyes, and red mouth, it sent him over the edge. He met her eyes in the mirror as he spilled himself deep, the orgasm going on and on. And he was whole again. They were one again.

CHAPTER 8

*J*osh plugged in his phone by his bedside and stripped for a nice warm shower. His phone had gone dead about three hours ago. He hadn't wanted to leave the water, but another team of volunteers rotated on duty, and he logically knew he had to rest. They'd agreed to let him sleep for a shift and come back in ten hours if they hadn't found the boy. Civilian fishermen were combing the waters as well. The Pie Maker had taken him off rotation for two days and the ferries weren't running. The crash had rocked the community. The captain of the primary ferry had made a judgment call. It had been a poor one. He was stuck in the position of trying to beat a storm while dealing with equipment failures. He'd been injured in the collision, and would lose his captain's license, but Josh felt sorry for him. After a long career on the water, he'd made a terrible mistake. He had to live with what had happened. People on both boats were injured and a little boy was missing at sea.

He saw his phone was flashing, and he checked his messages. One from Caitlyn with an update on Madeline. He was going to get five or six hours of sleep and then head over to the hospital. He had Katie's car now. When she found out he was riding in the rain on Tadgh's old motorcycle, she almost had a stroke. Given her history, he couldn't blame her. He checked his texts next. One from Michael, one from Seany, three from Charlie, and...*Jesus wept.* He had nineteen texts from Justine. Nope. He put the phone down, turned the light out, and fell asleep almost before his head hit the pillow. Just as he lost himself to sleep, he felt the swells of the ocean. A sensation that came from hours at sea. He wondered, fleetingly, if Madeline was feeling it too. Or if fatigue and medication had carried her into a peaceful oblivion. *Sleep well, Madeline.*

Twenty minutes later his phone rang. He'd sent a text to his family telling them he was going to sleep. They wouldn't be calling unless it was emergency. He answered, loopy with exhaustion. "What do you need, Justine? I need to sleep."

She bent his ear about not answering his texts until he interrupted. "For God's sake, don't you watch the news? I haven't been pub hopping, Justine. I've been out with the goddamn Lifeboat. I've been freezing my balls off pulling survivors out of the water and searching for a missing kid. I need some uninterrupted sleep, so you need to stop busting my nuts and give me some breathing room."

He ended the call, and he knew that she'd make him regret it. Right now, he didn't give a shit. As he drifted back off to sleep, all he could picture was Madeline hanging on to that little boy until Poseidon himself had come and ripped him from her arms. He felt a wave of sorrow and longing slide along his tired soul.

* * *

CORA WAS SO COLD. She'd never been so cold. It was very

dark. She could feel the jagged rocks under her elbow and tried to readjust. She was so scared. She looked down at her jeans, even as the leg did not belong to her. The rip was large, and the jagged cut the tear exposed was starting to throb. Then as if she'd split into two people, she asked, "How can I help you?" She'd never been able to do this before, but she wondered if her Aunt Miren had sparked something. A tool to maneuver through the scenes and people that came to her. She didn't understand. Was he dead? She felt a spike of fear for this boy, because it was a boy. She knew with certainty that this was the boy that Madeline had saved, and then lost with one swipe of the stormy sea. She could see him now. He didn't look good. "Show me something. Anything to help you. They told me you couldn't speak."

But they were wrong.

He didn't speak out loud, but it wasn't like she was standing before him in the flesh. She was inside him. Somehow, she'd breached his mind. It was an odd feeling. She'd felt her Aunt Miren do it to her, but this was different, somehow. He wasn't family and he wasn't an adult. He was her age, and he was a boy. As first dates went, this was a doozy. She felt his weakness and his low body temperature. She felt his desperation. She also felt his relief. He was relieved because he wasn't alone. The thought made her want to weep. She heard him, and in that moment, she was sure she'd never been so close to another person.

"I was pulled away from the woman, then I started to drift. Then I saw the shore." He wasn't Irish, but he wasn't quite English. "I'm inside the rocks. They cut into me and then they swallowed me whole." Then he shook violently as the sound of the crashing sea sent a spurt of sea water toward his feet. "I'm in the rocks." Then he drifted into unconsciousness.

* * *

FINN DRIFTED between sleep and wakefulness. He felt different. There was a hum in his mind. Like something coming to life. He smelled the ocean so clearly, he had to make sure he was awake. He smelled the sea and something else. Decaying seaweed and wet stone. He rolled into his wife, replacing the odd sensation with the smell of her hair.

Cora burst into her parents' room. She flipped on the light switch and looked, half stunned, at her parents. Luckily, they were partially dressed and under the covers now. His voice was groggy. "What is it, love? Another dream?"

She was almost afraid to say it out loud in case it wasn't true. "I think he's alive, Da. We've got to call Josh and Michael!" Because of course, no one else would believe them. And could you blame them? She barely believed herself when the dreams came to her. "I saw him, and he's alive."

* * *

JOSH DROVE Katie's old car to the hospital, finding the visitor parking. Mary was going to meet him in the main lobby and walk with him to Madeline's room. Her parents and sister hadn't left the hospital.

He walked into the lobby and Mary launched herself at him. "You saved her. Oh God, Josh. I can't believe this is happening."

"She's okay, Mary. Don't cry. You'll make me break down like a sissy and lose my street cred." He pulled back and smiled, and a little laugh escaped her as she wiped her nose.

She asked, "Any news on the boy?"

"No. I'm not going to lie, Mary. The longer he's missing, the less chance they'll find him alive or at all."

"Don't tell Maddie, okay? Just say you haven't heard any news."

They came to the door and he said, "When's the last time you ate?"

Mary said, "I don't know. My parents went to the cafeteria to call my grandparents and get something."

"Go join them. I got this. I won't leave her alone. Don't worry."

Mary looked at him with sad, knowing eyes. "You're a good man, Josh."

He went into the room to find her sound asleep. The sight of her hit him in the gut. Her lip was swollen where she'd bit into it, and there were dark stitches where they'd sewn the laceration. She was lucky, really. The fracture in her shoulder was going to heal. She was young and healthy. The nurse said, "She's sedated. She was having trouble falling asleep. She keeps talking about the little boy. Has he…"

Josh shook his head and her face fell. "She won't likely wake, but you're welcome to sit with her. She's going to be just fine. Are you a family member?"

"Not really. I just wanted to check on her. We're friends. I brought her in."

"A Yank volunteering with the National Lifeboat? That's a new one. Good for you, lad. A real hero, to be sure. I'll let you settle in. It's good to meet you." She prompted.

"Josh O'Brien. And thank you for taking care of her." The nurse left and he came farther into the room. He sat, suddenly wanting to weep. He took her hand and was so glad to feel the warm vitality of it. She'd been so cold when he pulled her out of the water. He never wanted to feel like that again. He put the back of her hand against his face. There was an IV in her arm, so he took great care with her. Treating her with as much gentleness as he could manage, given the intensity of his feelings. He turned her hand and kissed her wrist, right over her pulse. Then he prayed that when she woke, Rhys would be back in his mother's arms.

* * *

JOSH HATED LEAVING HER SIDE, but he needed to take the next shift on the boat. And deep down, he knew he didn't belong there. He'd made his appearance, which was proper. But he could get too used to being near that loving family. Too used to watching her sleep. As he pulled into the small boat dock on the Furbogh coast, his friend Ryan ran to him. "The Coast Guard wants us to start checking the sea caverns along the coast. They seem to think he may have crawled into one of them when the tide was low. Poor lad doesn't speak, so he can't yell for help. It's worth a try. You'll be on the D-class with me. We'll be combing the shoreline. There's a lot of nooks and crannies where the lad could have landed, if he's alive. It seems unlikely, though."

The boy was alive. He felt it in his bones. Then Cora had called him on the way over. Michael had been her first call. He was also headed back for another shift with the Coast Guard, this time on the boat that left out of the Doolin station instead of in the air. *When Cora tells you something, ye heed it.*

They worked efficiently, and Josh kept his water-resistant phone within earshot. The RNLI paged them on it, and he'd given Cora the number. She only saw things in her dreams, so it was unlikely the child would be able to go to sleep again. He didn't understand it all, but he hoped like hell she could give them something else. There was another round of foul weather headed their way, and a sea cave was dangerous when the tide came in. Time was not on their side. Especially with the water temperature being what it was. They left the dock, and he began instantly scanning with the search light as they skirted the rocky shore.

* * *

MIREN WATCHED her great niece pace the floor and wring her hands, wishing she could help. "Cora, remember what we tried in the doctor's office. Perhaps we could try again?"

Cora looked at her father. He'd been more than a bit put out he hadn't been consulted before Miren brought Cora into the bosom of the Colton Institute. He looked at Brigid, deferring to her. He was barely out of the doghouse.

Brigid said, "If you're sure, Cora. I know it's upsetting, and you need to prepare yourself." She knelt down next to her. "It's been hours, love. And that water is so cold."

"He's not in the water anymore. I can't explain how I know it; I just do. I saw it. I saw him." Brigid smiled at her, so proud that this fierce little ten-year-old was braver than any of them.

"Okay, let's do it," Brigid said.

Miren looked at Finn. "Do you feel anything?"

"No, not really. I mean, I feel like a weight has been lifted. I feel a bit of a hum. An awareness that I didn't have before. My head doesn't hurt even though I'm in the company of two witches."

"Da!"

"Just kidding," he winked. "And that would make me a warlock. Come to think of it, I like the idea of being a warlock."

Miren reached out her hand. "Just come and sit with us. If nothing else, you can watch Cora for any signs of distress. I am teaching her that sometimes, if she opens herself up in a relaxed state, then deep sleep isn't always necessary."

He hesitated. Old habits die hard, and he'd hidden this

part of himself for so long. Cora's voice was soft and under-standing. "It's okay, Da. You don't have to."

He did have to do this, he knew. He'd been by her side every step of the way. Even though he'd never told anyone about what had been done to him so many years ago, he'd supported her. That wasn't going to change. He sat quietly, and Brigid left the room to see to the boys and give them some quiet. A first, given her lifelong habit of jumping right into the middle of things.

Nothing happened for a long time. Miren helped them by slowly taking them into a relaxed, serene place. A sort of liquid existence like a pool of dark, comforting water. Eyes closed, there were no distractions. Finn was the first to sense something. The smell of the ocean was so strong. Not the smell you get from the beach, but richer. Seaweed and sand and live animals that clung to the rocks. It was so vivid. He almost felt the damp. Then another smell. It fouled the other scents. Old rubbish. Maybe discarded take-away. Ketchup packages? *What the hell?* He opened his eyes, looking around to see if anyone else smelled it, and everything was lost. Cora and Miren were gone, off on an unseen journey. He closed his eyes, and tried to reconnect to the sensation.

Cora felt the water on her feet. Her shoes were soaked, but the cold water was getting higher. She heard dogs. No, that wasn't right. It was a sort of barking, but it wasn't a dog. It was seals. More than one. She looked past the stone tomb that surrounded her, to the opening where she could see the dark night sky. She saw the clouds part briefly to reveal the yellow moon. He spoke then. Not with his mouth, but she heard him. *I'm so thirsty. I want to drink, but the salt. I just want some water. I'm so cold.* She wished she really was a selkie. She'd order those bloody seals to get in that cave and keep him warm. She'd swim to him herself. She tried to concentrate, trying to take in some other detail that would help her find him.

Her mind flashed backward. He was floating. It was earlier in the day. A memory of his, perhaps. She felt like he was helping her. Trying to show her the journey he'd taken. She saw the moment when he'd seen the shore was within his reach. He had a burst of energy. Fighting with strokes that were hindered by a bulky life jacket. Then she saw it through the blur of watery eyes. An old rusty trash bin. The ones placed near carparks in order to keep the litter out of the water. Then a cavern with a bottom that was a mix of sand and rock. He grabbed on, the rocks cutting his hand. He bounced up against it when a wave came cried out weakly as his jeans tore and he felt the rocks drag along the flesh of his leg.

Cora jerked back to herself. She was breathing heavily, having felt the panic and urgency of the boy's struggle. She actually felt along her thigh as if she was going to find that jagged cut. She looked at her father and her Aunt Miren. "The sea cave is near an old rubbish bin. It's an old, rusty, green rubbish bin like the type you see in carparks by the beach. Like when they were made out of metal instead of plastic. It's chained to a pole. It's not the real high cliffs, but there's a craggy drop off. And I think water's coming in! They have to hurry!"

Finn was in awe. "I smelled it. Not just the ocean and the stone, but I smelled old garbage. Jesus, it was so clear Miren. I smelled it."

She smiled, but she looked pale. It was like the effort had cost her something. She said, "That's how it was for you in the beginning. You smelled something as you drifted off to sleep."

* * *

CORA RODE SHOTGUN as her father drove along the coast path. "Cora, there's another storm coming. This is like looking for a needle in a haystack." She was on the mobile, hoping to God that Josh picked up. "He'd be past where they got Maddie. North of Galway. That's over an hour." He had his phone ringing on speaker, trying to get hold of Michael. When he picked up, Finn was ecstatic. Josh picked up a second later. They put them both on speaker and Cora told them what she saw. Every detail she could remember. "I heard seals. They were barking."

Michael said, "Christ, I think I might know where that is. It's not a carpark. If that's where I think it is, it's a small island off the coast between Ballyconneely and Lettermullan. It's a popular spot for kayakers to stop and search for shells or take a break. They take pictures of the seals and piss off the bull. That's the only one that has trash receptacles. We train in that area because of all the little islands. Christ, what is the name of it?" He thought for a minute. "Croaghnakeela Island!" He yelled it through the phone. "Inland is mostly beaches. That island is craggy, though. There's a little sea cave, not very large, and an unofficial campground. It's the only spot I can think of that has a cave and those old bins and there are definitely seals on the other side. Galway has a lot of beach strands, but if he was caught by that current, he could have gone toward that island instead of continuing toward the bay." He knew Josh was on the other phone. "Josh, your boat is closer, and the water is shallow, but I'm going to start that way. It's all we've got, so I'll keep the other boats on their normal search patterns and break away. I will try to send the air crew that way if I can. You call me if you get there first. The tide is coming in. This is going to be too close for comfort."

"I want to help, Michael!" Cora's voice was militant.

Josh said more softly, "You are helping, my sweet girl. But

you don't have wings or fins. The best thing you can do is go to Galway and wait until we call. Visit Maddie and sneak her some candy. Or just hold her hand. She's been really scared, and it might be good to give her parents a break. Can you do that?"

"Yes, I can." She looked at her dad. "Is it okay, Da? No school tomorrow." She looked so worried Finn didn't have the heart to tell her no. They were halfway there already.

"Galway it is," Finn said.

* * *

BRIGID PUT a cup of tea in front of Finn's aunt. Aideen had come over soon after they left. "Brigid called you, didn't she?" Miren said.

"She's right. You're pale, love. What is it? Are you sleeping?"

She smiled at her sister. "I am. Probably more than I should. I'm just enjoying not going to work. I'm enjoying being seaside again. Just let me be an old woman."

"You're not an old woman. If you are an old woman, then I'm an old woman. I refuse." Aideen's chin was up, openly defying father time.

Miren winked at Brigid. Then she said to her sister, "Are you angry I interfered with Finn?"

Aideen toyed with her cup. "No, sister. It's probably past time he dealt with those demons. He was so young. What he saw scared him. I did what I thought was best, but in hindsight, it wasn't best." She started tearing up. "I should have known. He was so sullen afterward. He thought I'd agreed to those tactics. And I sat in the bloody waiting area while they were hurting him. I should have stood up to mother. I should have stood up for you, too. There's nothing wrong with you, Miren. Is this why you came?"

"I knew I was needed. I didn't quite know why. Despite my air of competency, I don't actually know everything." They all three laughed.

Brigid said, "Cora and Finn are doing things that they couldn't do before. Is that because you're here? Are you, I don't know, enhancing them?"

She smiled, "Something like that. We're stronger together. We're of the same bloodline. And now Cora has Finn. She won't be alone anymore. The blood is strong in them both. The dark Irish from the McDubh side of the family. All sea dwelling tribes with the dark hair and eyes."

Aideen looked at her sister with such affection it almost made Brigid tear up. Things seemed to have healed somehow. Aideen said, "I always envied your coloring. That raven haired beauty appeal that drove the men wild. Even now, with the silver running through it, you look like some sort of high priestess."

Miren laughed at that. "A witch by any other name and all that? Hardly. I go to mass every Sunday; I'll have you know. Mother did do one thing right. But the Bible is full of people having visions. It just gets frowned upon when it's a woman. They loved strapping us to a stake or waterboarding us in the old days. Cora and I are lucky."

Aideen said, "She is a wonder, isn't she?"

"She is. And when the child grows into her full power as a woman, she will be glorious. The man who captures her heart will have to be something quite special."

Brigid, normally a chatter box, was content to listen to this exchange. But at that thought, she interjected. "She's an O'Brien as well. We have our own lore. She'll find her mate through trials and turmoil, but it will be forever. It's hard to think of my little girl falling in love, but it will happen."

Aideen took her hand. Then Miren put her hand over them both. "We'll be there to guide her; won't we?" Brigid concurred, but strangely, Miren said nothing. And her mask of serenity and confidence slipped for just a moment.

* * *

MADELINE WAS awake and feeling feisty. "I just want to go home." What she really wanted to do was help look for Rhys, and they all knew it.

"Well, Miss Nagle, that's all well and good, but we need to keep an eye on you for a little longer. Your body temperature is normal, but your oxygen levels need to come up a few more points. You aspirated sea water. Dry drowning is a very real thing. Do your breathing exercises and I'll see if we can round up some dinner. The doctor says you can take things by mouth now."

Madeline took her little breathing machine, sucking in and trying to hold the ball in the sweet zone. She scowled as she did it. With perfect timing to see her looking like an idiot, Phillipe walked into the room with flowers and an expression that looked like a repentant dog. He sat and took her hand. He looked over at her father sleeping on the lounge chair. He spoke quietly. "Madeline, I am so sorry this happened. I feel like a complete bastard for making you lead that tour."

"You are a complete bastard." She smiled as she said it, and he barked out a laugh. Her father stirred and then settled again. "But you know I don't blame you. The thought of it is ridiculous to your own ears, surely. It happened. I'm alive. We're all alive. At least, I hope so. I have to keep believing that this all happened for a reason."

"You mean the boy? The one from the tour. Yes, it is a tragedy. I have a little brother. Mon frère is not much older than le garçon." Phillipe always slipped into what they all called Frenglish when he was particularly stressed. She was tearing up, which she'd never done in front of anyone at the university. He smiled, "But you must be tired, ma chérie." He stood, kissing her on the forehead. That's when Cora and Finn walked in the open door, giving it a knock. Madeline was so stunned by the show of affection and the endearments, it took her a moment to register. Phillipe was involved with someone, she thought. Or maybe not, because he hadn't mentioned her recently. A woman from the history department. He was young and handsome, but she'd only ever seen him as Phillipe. The mentor, the fellow academic, and often the thorn in her side. She shook it off, because it was probably his guilt causing him to act out of character.

She smiled at Cora as she came running at her. The tears started coming back to her eyes in double doses. Finn said quickly, "Take care about the shoulder, Cora." That's when Madeline's father woke up on a snort.

Ronan said, "Who do we have here? This couldn't be the famous Cora?"

Cora had frozen mid-leap because she had forgotten about her injured shoulder. She shrugged shyly and said, "Hardly that. Are ye Maddie's da? I saw you at Caitlyn's wedding, maybe, but I was younger."

He took one of her hands and held it gently. "You're famous in my eyes. You're quite something. My Maddie and Mary have been telling me about how you helped the rescue swimmers find her, and that you're helping with the lad."

Finn watched the exchange and was so proud of Cora, it both touched and shamed him. How had someone so fierce come from the likes of him? But that was over now. He was not hiding anymore. It was hard for him to even remember why he'd been so adamant about not talking about it. He'd been a boy, and he'd suppressed the treatments because they'd been traumatic. Miren assured him that his mother would never have let them use pain tactics, and he really hoped so. He watched a strange look come over Cora as she looked at a tall, quiet man standing next to Madeline's bed. Madeline said, "Cora, this is my friend from school. His name is Phillipe."

Phillipe said graciously, "Hello, mademoiselle. Now what is this about you helping find Madeline?"

Madeline put up a hand. "It's a very long story for another time."

Cora said frankly, "You know Josh came to see you?" She looked at Phillipe and smiled her biggest smile, and only Finn knew that grin was pure Mullen. She was up to something. "Josh is the real hero. He's with the Royal Lifeboat and he saved Maddie. He dove out of the boat like a superhero and pulled her out of certain death. He's my cousin by marriage and he's American and gorgeous altogether."

Phillipe's brows shot up, message delivered. One side of his mouth lifted a tiny bit, but he didn't laugh. He just gave Madeline a sideways glance. "This Josh sounds like quite something. Now, Lady Cora, I must go home and get back to *ma chat*. She's been alone all day."

"Ye've got a cat? I like cats, but my da is allergic. We ended up with a fish. He's not very clever. What is your cat's name?"

"Lardons."

Maddie coughed as she started laughing, and it took a toll on her chest.

Ronan went to stand and she put a hand up. "I've got my wee machine, Da. Don't worry. Go on. This is getting good." She waved to Phillipe who had never told her he had a pet or the ridiculous name he'd given it.

"What is a Lardons? Is that French? It's an odd name for a cat. I bet he doesn't like it." Cora was admonished by Finn, but she didn't bat an eye. This was a stand off, and he thought it had something to do with her loyalty to Josh.

Interesting. He hadn't known there was a connection between the two.

"It's a she, and I don't think she minds. It's not a feminine name, I know, but she's not very ladylike. Lardons is the French word for pork fat or bacon. She was just a little, dirty thing. About four months old, maybe. She climbed in my window from the fire escape. I didn't notice until I saw her on the dining table, eating my carbonara. It's pasta with bacon, you see. I'd just paid more than was wise to have it delivered to my flat, and she stole it most ungraciously." His accent was getting thick as he told her the tale. That finally thawed her demeanor. She was a sucker for a good cat story.

"I think I'd like to meet your cat, but right now I'm busy." Then she changed lanes without a second glance. "Have you met Madeline's sister Mary? She goes to the university as well. You should tell Maddie to introduce you. She's very pretty and smart." She put her hand out and said, "It was nice to meet you, Phillipe. And don't worry, we don't blame you for making Maddie go on that boat." Then she turned and sat on the chair next to the bed.

The adults were captivated by the exchange, and Phillipe, being a gentleman, knew when to make an exit. He gave Madeline a chaste kiss, said goodbye, and left.

Madeline looked at the dark-haired child in front of her and was spellbound. She was an old soul, and she communed with the *taibhse*, the spirits that have passed on. Spirits or some would think the faeries. She would be stunning one day, when she came into her full womanly beauty. "Do I get another hug, now that you've scared off poor Phillipe?"

They held each other as the tears fell silently. Ronan left, nodding at Finn on the way out. "Is he alive, do you think?" Madeline's voice was sore from coughing and seawater and deep, deep, emotion.

Cora's head was to the side and a tear escaped and ran

into her hairline. "I don't know. He was weak from thirst and cold. So very cold. And he is hurt, Maddie. He's battered from getting thrown into the rocks. I just don't know how he's hanging on." Her voice was tight, the words painful. Then the tears came in full force. They both wept until they shook. "I could see you, Maddie. You were hanging on to him. It was so cold, and you tried so hard. I'm sorry I couldn't help you more. I wish I could have prevented the whole thing!"

"Cora, I don't know how it works, but I do believe you. And I think it all comes to you when it's supposed to. You aren't God. You can't stop a bloody-minded sea captain any better than you can stop a storm. I will never, ever be able to thank you, my love. You were like an angel looking over me at the darkest moment of my life." Her voice was strained, and she wept in Cora's hair. "And if he..." she hiccupped and tried to breathe evenly. "If he dies, then I'm glad he wasn't alone. I'm glad I was with him, and I'm glad you were with him. Even thought it will break both our hearts, I wouldn't trade it for anything."

She looked up into Finn's face and the tears streamed down his cheeks. He wiped them and nodded to her. "Thank you, Madeline. I think she needed to hear that."

CHAPTER 9

*I*t was so dark, now. Josh was grateful for the modern technology at his disposal in this RNLI rescue boat, and in the air. A helicopter had also shown up and was currently lighting up the water near the area where they needed to search. They had the air units situated in several key points on the western shore, everywhere from Galway to Sligo. There was no way the kid made it that far. The ferry had gone down not far from Inishmore, so the current very likely took him away from the bay and upward to the northern part of County Galway. The coastline was a series of peninsulas, beaches, and rocky spits. Craggy and unforgiving. If they didn't find him by morning, the odds were not in his favor. *Please, God. Don't take him. I am begging you to help me give him back to his parents.*

Josh didn't know how he was going to cope if the kid wasn't alive. Then with a surge of something like pride, he remembered his family. Not just Charlie, but the O'Briens. The ones who came to him at a time in his life when he was losing hope that he'd ever be whole and happy. The family was full of first responders and servants. His father had been a bum. A violent, drunk, piece of shit. He had that monster's blood in his veins, but he would not let that part of himself that was tainted ruin him. He'd follow the example of his new family. Even Aunt Sorcha, the small little grandmother, had tales of her bravery. If this child was in that cave, Josh would help take him back to his parents regardless of what condition he was in. It's no less than Michael, or Patrick, or Seany, or Tadgh, or any of the other amazing people he'd met would do.

* * *

MADELINE SHOOK her head when Finn tried to move Cora. Children often succumbed to sleep after a hard cry. She was feeling a little sleepy herself. "Let go, lass. Your parents went home to take showers. I'll keep watch."

"Wake me if you find out anything," she said, but she was drifting. Soon her breathing fell in rhythm with Cora's and they were both fast asleep.

Finn felt the warnings of a headache for the first time since he'd been to Wicklow. Cora's breath was faster now, and he knew she was dreaming. He remembered what the doctor had said. He'd been taught to suppress his gifts subconsciously, even beyond the hypnosis. He leveled his breathing, opening his mind and trying to keep the barriers down. There was a time when things had come to him on their own, but for some reason, Cora's own brain activity seemed to set him off, for lack of a better term.

According to the doctor, he might never get his abilities back, and that was okay. Not that he wouldn't love to help that lost child, but in the big picture he was okay where he was. He barely remembered what it was like to get those visionary dreams, so he didn't miss them. He felt no need to try for anything other than being free of those damn headaches. He just wanted to be here to help Cora, and he didn't want any lies between himself and his family. He closed his eyes, breathing deeply, feeling the hum of something not quite within his reach. And in the quiet, sterile environment of a hospital, he smelled the sea. The sea, and spongey green soil and moss. He smelled dried heather, past its season of bloom and left to dry and wither until next season. But that was all. He saw nothing but the backs of his eyelids.

Cora heard thumping, and the wind was so fierce. The water was almost filling the cave. She looked down at him. He'd crawled back as far as he could go to get away from the rising tide. He was so still. His eyes were shut. *No! You can't! You have to fight! Rhys! Wake up! The water is coming in!* Then she saw the light flash into what remained of the entrance. *PLEASE! Wake up, Rhys! It's Cora! I found you! They're here, but you have to wake up! You can't be dead!* The boy was so pale. Cora shot up in bed, gasping for breath. Her hand bit into Madeline's arm. Finn was out of the chair in flash. "Cora, I'm here. Deep breaths. Calm, lass. Be easy."

Madeline was staring at her in shock. "What is it? You fell asleep, darling. Was it a nightmare?"

"They've found him. You must call Michael." Even as she said it, she knew no one was going to pick their phone up in the middle of a rescue. Michael might be in the water, for all she knew. They'd have to wait. She thought about the boy's parents. They must be out of their heads. Cora looked at Madeline, tears welling in her eyes. "I don't know if he's alive. I couldn't tell. I'm so sorry."

* * *

JOSH DOVE INTO THE WATER, his swim buddy right behind him. It wasn't deep, about to his shoulders on a calm day. But the surge of the angry sea was warring with the incoming tide. That cave was almost full. Jesus, they couldn't be too late. Maybe it was a different cave? This coast was full of them. But somehow, he knew he was in the right place. Cora had seen this for a reason.

He submerged with a snorkel and mask and the water was a shock against his face, despite the neoprene hood. His dive light lit up the inside of the small little grotto. His heart stopped as he saw the still form of a boy who had crawled back as far as he could. "Rhys! Wake up, buddy. Oh, God please be alive!" He swam to the little body and didn't wait to find out. He grabbed the boy and clutched him to his chest. He was wet and pale and so still it scared Josh to even think about it. He backed out, having to time the swells so they had a sliver of opening left to swim out. At this point, one ill-timed splash in the face wasn't going to make or break this. He cleared the rocks, pulling on the tether that was tied to his boat. He thought he could hear his shipmates screaming, his swim buddy taking the boy's other side as he helped Josh suffer an incoming swell. They didn't want him smashing into the rocks with the boy in his arms. They got into the boat, put him on a backboard, covered him with everything they had on hand, and started checking for a pulse. That's when Michael's ship showed up just offshore where the water was deeper. Michael was on the radio. "I'm headed over in a small boat. Is he alive?"

"He's alive!" The medic from the RNLI teams screamed. "His pulse is weak but he's alive!"

They could hear cheering over the radio. Michael was there within five minutes with two other men. That's when the helicopter lowered its altitude and sent down the rescue basket. Michael and one other man put the boy in and Michael harnessed himself in with him. Josh watched in awe as they pulled them up to the helicopter, secured them, and made the lifesaving flight to the hospital.

* * *

It was Michael who made his way to Madeline's room first, as he had ridden in the helo with the boy. As he walked in the room, they all took in his face and body language. Fatigue and something else. Something that was a welcomed site. Relief.

Cora said without preamble, "He's alive." Not a question.

Michael marched over and scooped her off the edge of the bed where she sat. He hugged his niece so tightly, she squeaked. He whispered, his voice thick with emotion, "You are a miracle, a stóirín." *My little treasure.* "He's alive because of you."

"Da helped. So did Aunt Miren. It was the three of us," Cora said.

Michael put her down, looking down with a puzzled expression. Then he looked at Finn. Finn said, "Long story, brother. One worth telling, but not now. Right now, tell us about the lad."

He did. He was exhausted, so Finn gave him the seat where Ronan had slept. Madeline listened intently, wanting to hear everything.

"He was about twenty-five kilometers from the location where the boat went down. About seventeen from where Josh found you. The lad really went on a ride."

Madeline put her face in her hands and started to weep. "I tried to keep hold of him. I really tried."

Michael came to her, then. He'd known her since she was in braces and braids. "It's okay, lass. You kept him alive. His parents told us you put that life preserver on him right before the collision occurred. He would surely be dead if it wasn't for you. And you rode that current with him in your arms. It gave us a more specific direction to search for him. We all did this together, Madeline. And Josh pulled three people out of the water on his first real run."

She put her head up and met his eyes. "Josh was the one that found him?"

He smiled. "He's an O'Brien. He was the first one in the water. He pulled that lad out of that cave minutes before he'd have drowned. The boy had succumbed to hypothermia and was unconscious, but he's slowly coming out of it. This day is full of heroes." He kissed the top of her head. "Josh should be here soon. They need to put the equipment away and then he'll want to come see the boy. They were going to fly him to Dublin to be treated at the PICU, but decided they could handle his care here. He's a tough kid. He was already coming around in the bird."

She thought of his sweet face. Dark eyes and hair, not unlike Cora and Finn's. His parents were Welsh to the core. Excitable, making cracks about the English with their clipped, sing song accents, sharp witted but also fun and kind. And they adored their son. They spoke to him like he was normal in every way. Used basic ASL when more in depth conversations needed to happen. According to them, there was nothing physically wrong with him. He suffered only from selective mutism. An anxiety induced disorder where the child simply stopped speaking, even though they were capable of it. The trauma he'd witnessed at five years old was probably the culprit. She was so happy and relieved for them it welled up from her heart. Her body couldn't contain it, so she wept in great heaving sobs. So did Cora. "He's alive, my sweet girl. You did it. You all did it."

The room went silent, and she looked up to see Josh in her doorway.

* * *

GUS O'CONNOR'S **Pub**
Doolin, Co. Clare, Ireland

The pub was quiet on a weekday, being close to closing. It was a bank holiday tomorrow, but the mood was sedate. Many had gone up the coast to help search the coastline for the missing boy. Some took their boats out, if they could tolerate the weather. Gus's was giving free meals to the shifts of men and women who would come back after a cold few hours. They'd come in a group at a time, exhausted and sad. There were only about thirty people in the pub right now, and the trad session was over. Musicians were packing up. That's when the call came in. Jenny shouted to occupants, her voice cracking with the effort. "They found him! They found the boy and he's alive!" The group was on their feet cheering and hugging! The relief sweeping over the whole place.

She looked over at the quiet, strong man who'd been nursing a pint of lager. He was talking with Liam O'Brien. They'd both taken a shift and come in together. Seamus O'Keefe was a doctor up near the university who'd done a medical mission with Liam. He was a fine looking man. About ten years older than herself, but a kind and funny fort of man that made him seem younger. And he was divorced. She slid another pint in front of him and Liam. She didn't want to seem too obvious, after all. "That one is on me, lads."

Seamus smiled at her, then said to Liam, "I'm going to have to sleep on Patrick's couch with you tonight."

Liam laughed. "If an Irishman can't handle two pints of lager, he needs to move out of the country."

I'd give him a place to sleep tonight, Jenny thought. But she never said anything. No way. He was a doctor, for God's sake. She was a barmaid from a small town. She'd never been anywhere. She hadn't even gone to college. She wasn't stupid. She read everything she could get her hands on. She didn't even own a television. But Dr. Seamus O'Keefe was way out of her league.

He said, "Thank you, Jenny. For the beer and the good news. It's been a long day. It's good to get a happy ending." He winked at her and she almost knocked an empty glass over as she started wiping the bar down for no reason. Liam's smirk made her realize he knew. The little bastard knew. She was going to strangle him when she got him alone, just for that smirk. She saw another tall figure come in and said, "We just had last call!" That was before she recognized Seany.

"It's all right, love. I'm knackered. Just a Coke, if you don't mind." She poured him a Coke and slid it across the bar as he sat next to his brother. "It seems I've missed all of the action."

"Aye, you did. Have you had any action on your side of the country?"

"Blissfully quiet. Cats in trees and the like. So, Josh had his mettle tested, I hear. Damn. What a first call. I'm glad it all worked out. I'm headed up north to see Maddie as soon as I check in with Mam. She's got some stuff for the new house and demanded I visit. I'll head up after a cup of tea."

"Do you want me to drive? I can forgo this one." Liam motioned to his pint.

"Nah, I'll be grand with a bit of caffeine. I took a final nap on the floor before I left that apartment for good."

"I'll miss having you as a neighbor." Liam clinked glasses with him. Liam had lived in Dublin before Brazil. Seany had given up their apartment to move in with Patrick and Caitlyn when Liam had gone off the grid and never come home. Tadgh had lived above them, then Tadgh, Charlie, and Josh made three. When Patrick and Caitlyn moved back to Doolin with their children, Seany and Josh took over that apartment. Then when Liam came home with Izzy for good, leaving Arizona, they'd taken over Tadgh and Charlie's apartment so they could move out of the city, and he and Izzy were still there. A merry-go-round of O'Brien occupants and subleases because the digs were in a great location. It was too bad that Seany and Josh had to go. The good news was that he found a set of married doctors to rent it, so he wasn't going to have douchebags above him.

"How is Madeline, really?" Seany directed the question to Seamus.

"She's going to be just fine. The shoulder will heal. My guess is they'll let her go home tomorrow if her O2 stats are stable. They like to watch people overnight when they get cases like hers. She aspirated seawater, and she was hypothermic. Not as bad as the poor lad, but still. Better safe than sorry. She'll need a sling."

The relief on Seany's face was visible. Liam said, "Are ye sweet on her, Seany?"

"No, Jesus. She's like family. I've known her since I was in short pants. But I know someone else who was probably out of his head for a bit."

Liam gave a grunt of understanding. "And he was the one to find her. That's good. That's really good. Will anything come of it, do you think? With Maddie, I mean?"

"Two stubborn goats. Who the hell knows?" Seany said, half disgusted, half joking.

"Aye, so what you're saying is he fits right in with the rest of the O'Brien men." Seamus said it and then casually sipped his beer. Jenny barked out an unladylike laugh, and he gave her another wink.

Liam laughed too. "Touché, brother. We sort of walked into that one."

CHAPTER 10

UNIVERSITY HOSPITAL GALWAY

inn knew when to make an exit. So did Michael. They exchanged glances as Cora ran to Josh and hugged him. The raw pain and desire on the young man's face was enough to take them back a few years. They knew that gut-wrenching pain. The want, the fear, the sheer stubbornness that made a simple thing like falling in love really fucking hard. Michael slapped him on the back. "Well done, brother. If you get citizenship, I might poach you from that lifeboat and put a uniform on you."

Josh laughed, but inside he was warm pudding. The site of Madeline sobbing over that little boy was like a kick in the nuts. They all made a hasty exit in order to grant them a bit of privacy, no doubt. Josh met her eyes. They were full of tears. She croaked. "Get over here! I'm all hooked up and tangled in this damn bed! Get over here right now!" She shouted, which should have startled him because she was such a mild-mannered woman. But she was raw and had to have felt really helpless being shackled to a hospital bed. Instead he laughed and followed orders. She clutched him so tightly he melted into her. "You did it. You found him. It was you who found him. Oh, God Josh. Thank you."

She sobbed against his neck and he pulled her closer, feeling the tears prick his eyes. A surge of male protectiveness and possessiveness coursed through him to the point where it almost scared him. His heart was pounding. He kissed her head all over, not wanting to let her go. Then his hands were in her hair and he was kissing her eyes. Her hair was long and thick. Someone had cleaned her up, washed the sea from her body. She was so alive. So warm. "Madeline. You're okay. Finding you like that in the water was a nightmare. You were so cold and weak. Jesus." He kept kissing her temples and then her eyes again. "And he was so still. I was afraid I was too late." She had both hands on the side of his face.

"It's okay. You saved us both." Their noses were close, their foreheads together. All he had to do was close the distance and fuse their mouths. It would be so easy.

His savior and his executioner wore nurse's scrubs. She was in the door with her paper cup of meds and her iPad before she saw the two of them embraced. He pulled away, cursing to himself about how far he'd taken that embrace. Cursing the nurse for interrupting before he'd finally tasted Madeline Nagle's mouth. She said, "Oops, sorry. Do you want me to come back?"

Yes, and lock that door on your way out, Madeline thought. She'd been in his arms. She'd felt his hands in her hair. His mouth on her skin. Had it been the relief of the moment? Probably, but she didn't care. It had been electric.

"No, don't apologize. Please, I have to leave anyway." He turned to Madeline and almost groaned out loud. Her cheeks were flushed and her eyes were alive with something. Those deep, grey-green eyes that looked like the dark and stormy sea. "I just needed to see you for myself. I'm going to go find Rhys's parents. Michael and the doctors are talking to them right now. I'm sure they'll want to see you, if that's okay?"

She nodded dumbly. When he left, the nurse actually craned her neck to watch his butt. "Wow. I can't even apologize to you enough, right now, can I? Sorry about the cock block but it's time for your vitals. I hope you have his number."

Maddie almost growled at her.

MICHAEL'S HEART lurched in his chest as he saw the two parents huddled over their young son. He was still in his Coast Guard utilities, and when they looked up, the mother said, "Are you the one who found him?"

Before he could answer the woman launched herself at him. Then the father was there. Both dark like their son, she was a sprite of a thing. He was tall and lean. He patted the woman, uncomfortable at her praise. He wasn't the hero of the day. At least, not the main one. "You're welcome. I have three of my own. Two sons and a daughter. We all wept for you, and we prayed. He stepped back from them. "And to answer your question, no. I was not the first one on the scene, nor did I pull him out of the cave."

"Cave? I'm sorry," the father's throat convulsed. "I think we should sit down. In lieu of a stiff drink, I'm going to need a chair."

Michael led them to the closest sitting area. They listened as he explained where exactly they'd found his son. As he saw Josh ambling down the hallway in search of them, he gestured. "This is the lad of the hour. He's with the Royal National Lifeboat Institute. He was the first in the water to pull Madeline Nagle out, then the first to go into that sea cave for your son. If he hadn't found Madeline, he may never have found your son."

"I don't understand," the mother, Abigail, said softly. It was a bit confusing.

Josh knelt down in front of the mother. "It's a long story. But I'll start by telling you that Madeline Nagle, your tour guide, landed not far from your son in the water. I believe they were both thrown clear because she was standing, and he was so lightweight. She stayed with him, Ma'am. She held onto him for miles until the sea ripped him from her arms. They got caught in a current that pulled them north. She clung to him like a mother bear with her cub until the moment when he was torn from her arms. She's been beside herself."

The boy's mother listened as she covered her mouth. The father took a shuddering breath. "We were able to track his direction based on where we found her. He drifted another seventeen kilometers."

"I don't understand, even given the general direction, how in the bloody hell you found him inside a cave. We've been combing maps, driving for hours. It was too rough for us to be allowed on your boats, but we still drove. It was nearly impossible. All of those beaches and coves and little islands. What sort of Gods do you have on your side that you found our son seventeen kilos north, on an uninhabited island, inside a bloody sea cave? It's impossible!"

What God's indeed, Michael thought. He looked at Josh, weighing the lunacy of telling the truth. The mother said, "I see it in your eyes. You're not telling us something." Her Welsh accent was clipped and demanding. "I would hear it all. If there's another that deserves my gratitude, I'd hear it all."

* * *

MICHAEL TOOK the parents back to the room, and they paused in the doorway as the vision of a beautiful child stood beside their son's bed. She held his hand, speaking softly to him. Michael nodded at him, answering the unasked questions. This small young girl had been their salvation. "I can't believe it. It's not true, surely," the father said.

Michael said softly, "Is Wales so far removed from its old magic? Have the old ones abandoned you altogether?"

The hair stood up on Josh's arms as Michael spoke the words. English, but in a tongue that was barely so. His accent thick, his tone admonishing.

The father of this boy, Rhys Sr., nodded his head. He was dark like his son. "Aye, my grandmother used to say she got feelings when something was about to happen. Said she felt it in her bones."

They watched in amazement as the boy finally opened his yes. They moved in as he squeezed Cora's hand. She looked to them. "You're his mammy and his da," she said. But not really a question. She smiled. "I just wanted to tell you…" She looked at the boy. "He's in there. He may not speak, but he's in there. He's trying to come back to you." The boy's mother let out a stifled sob as her husband supported her against him.

And then something happened that shocked everyone, including the mute child who had been so still in the hospital bed. He said one word. "Cora." Cora gasped. She hadn't told him her name. Not with words. But they'd communicated. And at the end, she'd shouted for him to get up. And in her mind, as she tried to insert her will into that cave, trying to reach across the space between them…yes, she'd given him her name right at the end. *Wake up, Rhys! It's Cora!*

The parents gasped as well. He hadn't spoken since the day of the accident. Since the day the boy had grabbed at his mother, yanking her back before any forewarning. With all of the strength his five year old body could possess, thirty seconds before catastrophe, he'd yanked her out of the pedestrian crossing. While she chastised him on the sidewalk, that accident had occurred, brutally and fatally before their eyes. And he'd never spoken again.

"Cora," he repeated. His voice was raspy from sea water, but it was clear enough.

Cora looked down at the lad she'd grown so close to, but only just met. She'd been inside his mind. And that idea made her feel funny as she looked down at him. He was a handsome boy, though pale and weak. Dark eyes and hair, like the selkies of her own island. But the Welsh were Celts as well. "Rhys, I'm glad you're back. I've been waiting to meet you," she said softly as the tears fell down onto his blanket.

* * *

MADELINE WAS SO glad to be freed from her hospital bed. She was going to be released in about six hours when the doctor did his rounds. It was late, but she found an ally in her sister. Mary had returned soon after Josh's departure, and she came with information. The boy, Rhys, had not been transferred to the PICU in Dublin. He was stable and his injuries were surprisingly mild given the journey he'd been on. He'd been stung by a jellyfish on his ankle, but it hadn't been a particularly nasty one. He was suffering from severe dehydration and hypothermia. They'd sedated him for the worst of it, as they had her. The process of your numb hands and feet being brought back up to a normal temperature could be uncomfortable. She still felt some lingering nerve pain in her toes, but she could walk. They'd encouraged her to do so as long as she had someone with her.

Rhys had been admitted to her floor, because the pediatric floor was full of victims of a particularly nasty H1N1 influenza. Because she and so many of the passengers had aspirated sea water, the infection protocol was high. No nurses who were working the pediatric floor were allowed to work with compromised patients. She didn't feel compromised, but it had kept Rhys out of pediatrics, hence this little walk down the hall to "stretch her legs."

"So, I heard Josh came by tonight," Mary said, trying to keep her tone light.

"Cora told you, I suppose," she said with a grin.

"Yes, she'd make an excellent spy. Down to the facial expressions she observed when you both saw each other." Mary said, her tone going from light to teasing.

She didn't comment, because she was at the door and she saw him. His parents were on either side of him, and they looked so tired. Their faces shifted as they both recognized her. The mother got to her first. She took Madeline's hand. "Oh, Abigail. I'm so sorry. I tried to keep hold of him." The tears started immediately, and she couldn't control them as the relief and regret rolled through her chest in great sobs.

Abigail held her gently, watching her injuries. "You're wrong to be sorry, love. The wrong sort might have taken his life jacket and left him to die. You held on to him like a mother bear. I heard it all, pet. From the rescue swimmers and from little Cora."

Madeline pulled back, wiping her face. "You've met our Cora?"

"I have. And they've left me with the sure knowledge that I couldn't have done more myself. And don't forget, I watched you put that jacket on him. He'd been so adamant, and I brushed him off. I think…I think he knew."

She remembered then. He'd been a bit panicked and was trying to put a lifejacket on himself and his mother. She met the woman's eyes, and Abigail repeated, "I think he knew."

She raised her brows in surprise, then looked at the sleeping boy. "You think he's like Cora?"

"I don't know. All I do know is that two times that child has saved me from tragedy and certain death. It was mere seconds after I'd acquiesced and put that life jacket on that the collision happened. His father's a good swimmer, but I would have been done for. One tragedy plunged him into silence. The other brought him out of it."

"What do you mean? Ye don't mean he spoke?" Madeline was shocked. "What did he say?"

"He said, *Cora.* It's quite a connection. I'm not ashamed to admit, the hair on the back of my neck stood up. I've never seen the like. He looked at her like he knew her. And, how could he? But he said her name, and when he looked at her it was like he…"

"What?"

"Like he knew her. Like he'd always known her. It frightened me, a bit. His father left the room. He couldn't take it. Hearing the boy speak like that… he just needed a minute. It was so much to take in. The whole business. He spoke, Madeline. The boy spoke."

CHAPTER 11

DOOLIN, CO. CLARE

*C*ora sat in the extra wide chair-and-a-half with her Uncle Seany and sighed wistfully. Rhys was gone. She'd wanted to drive to the airport, but his parents hadn't wanted an emotional rehash of the last few days, so they'd gone like a storm that just drifted out to sea. They hadn't even given her contact information. They'd been gracious in every other way, but they were scarred by the near death of their son. The loss. The waiting. The crippling fear. So they'd left Ireland behind them and returned back over the Irish Sea. Would she ever see him again? Did it matter? Probably not, but she'd never met any other kid who was sensitive like her. And she wasn't positive, but she thought that maybe he was. Maybe the trauma of his early visions had caused him to retreat into that world of silence.

Her Aunt Miren came into the room and she smiled, getting up to greet her. She went into her aunt's arms, letting her scent invade her nose. Her Granny Sorcha had just left, bringing over sweets to soothe the emotional upheaval of the last few days.

"Granny Aideen came to me last night. We had a long

117

talk. She was so proud of me and of Da. She told him so. He doesn't do what we do, but he's starting to learn again."

"He may never be able to, Cora. It was locked away for so long. And some children outgrow it. He might always be sensitive in some ways, but he may not be able to call forth the sight like we can."

"Can I? I mean, you were doing a lot of it weren't you? I felt you."

"Aye, I was. But you never know. Maybe someday you won't be at the mercy of your dreams and will be able to do it on your own." Miren said.

Cora thought she was so wise and beautiful. She'd seen pictures of her from her youth. She'd been a stunning woman. Long, raven hair and lively eyes. "Will I look like you when I'm older? Will I be beautiful?"

"Darling, you're already beautiful. How could you doubt it?" Miren looked at Seany to weigh in. He'd kept silent, pretending to read, but he'd been listening. Cora looked at him, too.

Seany said, "Cora, my sweet lass, the entire force of the O'Brien clan is going to have to keep the young lads in their place. They'll be making honey in their hearts, begging you for your hand."

Brigid's voice came behind them. "Aye, and I'll beat the wee mongrels with my fists if they get any ideas about my baby girl."

Cora rolled her eyes. "Mam, ye can't go beating people up. And it's not like any boys look at me now. Jenny McBreed and Darlene Connel keep telling everyone I'm a witch and that I'm going to get a wart on my nose."

Her little brother Colin came in the room just in time to hear. He wrapped his arms around Cora and said, "If they were boys, I'd kick them up the arse!"

Seany spit his coffee all over his magazine. "I know Finn didn't teach him that."

Brigid stayed focused on her daughter, not arguing the point. "Screw those little shrews. You've got Jessica and Aisling on your side, right? Don't you eat lunch with them every day?" As soon as the words were confidently spoken, Brigid's face fell at Cora's silence.

She came all the way into the room. "Cora, who do you eat lunch with everyday?" Cora's face turned pink with shame and Brigid said, "Tell me, love."

"I eat alone and then sit in the library during recess."

"Why has no one told me this, Cora?" Brigid's face was shattered. "Why, my darling?"

"Because it's no crime to read a book instead of subjecting myself to Jenny and Darlene using their mother's pink sea salt to put rings of protection around themselves and their friends. They think they're very clever." Then the corner of her mouth tipped up, just like her father's when he had a mind for mischief. "When I walked right into the ring and shouted a hex at them, the lunch aide suggested maybe I'd like to read in the library during lunch."

Miren and Seany burst into laughter at the same time. "Well done, lass!" Miren said. Brigid was furious of course, threatening to ring the neck of the completely incompetent lunch aid who just happened to be Jenny McBreed's second cousin.

You couldn't follow your kids to school. And after a certain age, you couldn't fight their battles for them. You could coach, empower, even cry with them, but from some things you couldn't protect your child. And every adult in the room hated that fact.

* * *

119

Josh spent a beautiful day on the water's edge. Eeragh Lighthouse seemed to be on the edge of everything, and Pete was a good teacher. Today, Josh learned how to replace a solar panel that had been damaged during the storm. He'd needed the day to shake hands with the sea. It had been like a living, breathing enemy for a small time, although the notion was foolish. Now the sun was low in the sky, leaving his cheeks pink and his clothes damp with salt prickling the skin on his arms. Charlie was at Katie's today. Seany was headed home from Dublin, and they'd drive into Galway together.

He cursed as he pulled into his driveway and saw Justine's car. He'd seen very little of her over the last two days. She'd met him out for a bite to eat and he'd told her all about the rescues. She'd been uncommonly quiet. He thought about the tear-soaked phone call his sister had made that next morning, telling him he was a hero and how proud she was. Justine's words had seemed begrudging and flat. Even a little bitter. *Aren't you just the local hero? Maybe they'll forgive the fact that you're a Yank if you save enough of the local girls.* Of course, she'd latched onto the details about the woman he'd pulled out of the water, all but ignoring the fact he'd saved a little boy. She didn't know who the woman was, luckily.

"Justine, how are you? Come on in. I'm going to need a shower, but I have a little time to spend with you. Seany and I are headed into town to see my granny."

He noticed, then, that she had a beer bottle in her hand. "Isn't your granny in Iowa?" She took a final swallow of her beer. She liked to get a jibe in now and again about him not being a real O'Brien. Her nasty side reared its ugly head when she'd had a few too many.

"Ohio not Iowa, and I didn't mean that grandmother. I meant Granny O'Brien. I know she's not my real grandmother, but she cares for me more than the two in Ohio ever did. Have a seat." He motioned to the chair. "Do you want some tea or coffee?"

She sneered and he couldn't for the life of him figure out why she was upset. "Such a gentleman. When were you going to tell me, Josh? I saw the news report. The woman you pulled out of the water was the one who showed up and interrupted the perfectly good fuck we were getting ready to have."

Dread washed through him. "I'm not sure what kind of response you're expecting." He sighed, rubbing his eyes. "I like you, Justine, but…"

She cut him off. "Surely you don't think it will work with someone like her? She'd take you for a ride, yes. But she's not going to settle for a lad with your past and lack of prospects. You're broke. You can't even afford a decent house," she said, motioning around herself. "You wait tables in a pie shop. But you and I understand each other, love. I understand about having a drunk for a father."

She sidled up to him, running her hand through his hair. He felt the despair wash over him. Not because she'd said the hurtful words, but because he knew she was right. He was tainted because he'd been sired by a violent alcoholic. Not the *grab a woman by the elbow and break some dishes* type of garden variety wife beater. He was a monster. He'd actually taken a hot iron to Charlie's back. He'd permanently scarred her while Josh had cowered in his bedroom. *Go to your room, Josh. Don't come out no matter what you hear.* She'd shielded him and taken the full force of their father's wrath.

Then there were the nights he'd knocked his mother around. The muffled sounds they made…as he'd raped her. Josh shook himself, feeling sick. It was the first time he'd even dared to confront that word, even in his own mind. His father was a brutal, wife-abusing monster. Verbal abuse, financial abuse, emotional abuse, physical abuse, and there had been sexual abuse. The sound of his father forcing himself on his petite mother. *You think you can tell me no?* And his mother's pleas. *Don't do this, please. Just let me sleep on the couch. You're drunk.* Then a slap, and his mother's muffled cries as she hit the bed. He'd been about fourteen the last time he'd heard it. Old enough to step in. His father had gotten nose to nose with him. Then when Josh turned to walk away, he punched him right in the kidney. He'd pissed blood for two days, but there would be no doctor's office for him.

His mother was a walking ghost, and he'd started sleeping nights at his friends' houses. With Charlie gone, he'd played the dangerous game of avoiding his father's fists. His mother had refused to leave him, though, no matter what he'd done to her.

Josh pushed away from Justine. He might not deserve someone like Madeline, but he couldn't do this right now. He couldn't be touched right now. Not by anyone. But she persisted, her hands fumbling to get under his shirt. "Justine, stop! Okay? I need you to give me some space." He could smell the beer on her breath, her dark hair filling his nose because it smelled like smoke. Like a bar.

Her mood switched in a flash. She yelled, "Space? Do you think you're going to reject me? Just shag me and dump me like some whore?"

Josh said, hands splayed, "Would you calm down. That's not what I'm saying."

"Fuck you!" In hindsight, he should have been worried about the bottle. She had a bad temper. She'd shoved him a few times, lost her temper and tore into him. But he honestly hadn't thought she'd go over the line this badly. The bottle smashed behind his left ear, pain searing through his skull. He fell to his knees and she gave one parting shot. "You have no idea how much trouble I can make for you."

He felt his head, and the blood was warm and sticky. He was mindful on some level that there was broken glass everywhere. He lifted himself with one arm on the coffee table just as he heard her car start and go into reverse. He didn't hear Seany come in because he must have pulled in as she was leaving.

"Jesus Christ, Josh!" Seany's voice was panicked. He looked behind himself, his head swimming with the effort. There was a lot of blood. Then everything started to dim. Seany pulled a chair out and under his butt before he fell over. Then he was on the phone, calling emergency services.

"I don't have insurance. You can't call an ambulance. I'm trying to get citizenship!" He knew he was being irrational, but suddenly it seemed important. "I can't leach off the system!"

Sean said harshly, "I'm going to strangle that little psycho! Just stay seated, for the love of God, brother." He spoke to the operator. "White male, twenty years of age, laceration to the left side of the scalp, behind the ear. Possible glass shards imbedded, bleeding, unsteady on his feet, suspected concussion. He was assaulted with a beer bottle. The assailant has fled the scene." The next call was to Tadgh, and Josh actually tried to get up and take the phone from Seany. Charlie was extremely pregnant. She couldn't know about this for more reasons than he could count, but he just couldn't seem to balance himself and planted back down on the chair.

UNIVERSITY HOSPITAL GALWAY

Josh's head was pounding. He'd been given lidocaine in order to tolerate the sewing, but he was in a bad way. He must have shown signs of distress, because the nurse had a plastic bin in front of him just as he tossed up the remainder of his PB&J from lunch. Seany came back into the curtained-off area. "You've got to see her, Josh. She's out of her head sitting in that waiting room."

"Does she know what happened?" He sounded so sad, it almost made Seany tear up.

"She does. I'm sorry, Josh. I'm not going to keep this from her. Given your history, this is something Charlie's going to be able to understand better than me."

"It's not the same. What happened tonight is not the same." Josh said.

"You've never told me it all, so I can't comment, but right now you need your sister." He moved to open the curtain, then he motioned to someone. Charlie waddled in and suddenly he was so ashamed. "I'll give you two some privacy."

* * *

"I DON'T UNDERSTAND THIS, Josh. How could you get involved with someone like this?" The sadness in Charlie's voice made him want to throw up again.

"She never did anything like this before. It just got out of hand. She'd been drinking and she was upset." Josh hated that he had to make excuses for her.

She stood, hands on hips, looking at him so intensely that it unnerved him. Her eyes welled up with tears. "Are you listening to yourself?" She covered her faced and scrubbed it with her palms, then looked blankly, "I can't believe this is happening again. What did you do when she hit you?"

"Bled."

"I'm serious, Josh! Did you fight back?"

"I would never hit a woman. I'm not Dad, for God's sake!" He winced at the pain in his head.

She moved in closer, making him hear her words and

meet her eyes. "Is that what you think? That I'm comparing you to Dad? Jesus, Josh! You are nothing like him. I'm afraid this might be worse. You aren't Dad. Don't you see, Josh? You're Mom. You've made excuse after excuse for her bad behavior, her jealousy and anger, and her violence. You are Mom!"

He shook his head and then instantly regretted it. "I'm done with her. It was only a few weeks and I'm done, okay? I won't see her again."

"It's past that, honey. Tadgh already called the local Gardai. They are arresting her when they find her. And you will not fight me on that, Josh."

He sighed, feeling very unsteady even sitting up. "I didn't know her that well. I'm not emotionally invested. If you want her arrested, then I won't interfere."

"You should want her arrested! That's my whole point!" She rubbed her abdomen, feeling a stitch. Before he could stand up, she said, "I'm okay. It's just a twinge. Focus on this."

"I understand why you're upset. I do, Charlie. I was going to break it off anyway. She was bad news."

Charlie sat, done ranting and ready to talk. "Seany told me everything. There were warning signs she wasn't stable and that she had an ugly side. I'm afraid, Josh, because not only did you not see those red flags, but you stayed with her when they were pointed out to you. Kids who grow up in houses like we did often end up with abusive spouses."

"Or they end up being the abuser. That's the other part of that story you don't want to think about. That sons imitate their fathers. I've never been in love, Charlie. I was too busy trying to survive to be a normal kid. Swim team was all I had. I was too embarrassed to have other kids over. So, I've never had the passion that comes with really being in love. I don't know what kind of partner I'd be if I was really invested. What if there is a sleeping dragon inside me?"

Charlie was crying now. Silently, she wept at the fear in his voice. Fear that their father had begot a monster just like himself. She hated her father, right now. "Just because you're male and I'm female doesn't mean only you have to worry about it. Do you think I didn't have shit to work through with Tadgh? My first serious relationship, the guy was a controlling dickhead." Josh remembered. He'd despised the jerk. "You can't have shallow relationships based on sex or hang out with women who are morally not your equal just because we had a rough upbringing. You are worthy of a good mate, just like me. We have to believe it, or what was the use of surviving it all?"

Josh shut his eyes. "You don't understand, Charlie. I was there for years after you left. You don't know how bad it got. It wasn't just the physical stuff. You don't know what a coward I was. The kind of stuff that went on while I hid in my room!" He wiped his face; the effort of fighting his tears causing his jaw to ache along with his head. "I am tainted by him."

She reared back, shocked at such a statement. He was her beautiful boy. He was like an angel. She'd known it from the first time he was put in her arms. Always so sweet and giving. Her father never knew how to handle him because he was too good. "How could you say that about yourself? Do you think I'm tainted?"

"No," he said softly. A tear leaked down his cheek and it gutted her. He smiled sadly at her. "You were the hero in this story, Charlie. You got us both out." She put an arm around him, and he shuddered, needing the warmth she offered.

Charlie was undone the moment he was in her arms. He needed this and so did she. She didn't hold him enough. "My sweet boy. Oh, God. My angel. I can't stand that she hurt you!"

"I love you Charlie. I'm sorry about this whole thing. And

now I'm on the radar with the police. Justine could say anything. She could say I hit her or something equally awful. She could claim she was just defending herself. They could deport me. Plus, the medical bills. I could have very well just ruined everything with my screwed up choices."

Tadgh spoke from the opening in the curtain. "The bill is taken care of already. Your grandmother paid it without batting an eye. She was visiting with Mam for the day when this happened. And before you argue, she can afford it. If she hadn't paid it, someone else would have stepped up. We take care of each other in this family." He used the pronoun *your* when he talked about Granny Aoife because Josh needed to know that they were one family. He belonged. He could claim the name O'Brien and everyone who went with it. He thought about Josh's concerns with regard to immigration.

Tadgh cursed under his breath. "I should have adopted you. I shouldn't have depended on the student visa. I'm sorry. Jesus, Josh. I'm so sorry about all of this. You shouldn't have this residency thing hanging over your head along with everything else. But maybe this will all blow over."

Tadgh came further into the room and gave him a quick squeeze. "You can go home, but you need to be monitored. Any vomiting, fever, worsened pain, you need to come right back. The guards will want a full account, Josh. And don't sugar coat it. The best way to cover your ass is to tell the truth in as much detail as you can. The fact that you just saved an Irish citizen and a tourist in one day is not going to hurt when you are compared to this Justine woman. No one is going to let this blow back on you. You were the victim. I know that word gives you the scratch, but that's just police talk. It's not meant to insult you. Now go home and let Seany take care of you, okay?"

Josh stood up, Charlie taking one arm and Tadgh taking the other. An older nurse stood by with a wheelchair. "Rules are rules. Plant your bum, lad." As he watched his sister go ahead of him at a full waddle, his heart squeezed. She was going to be such a wonderful mother. She'd mothered him at a time in his life when his mother had retreated into herself and couldn't care for anyone. She was saying something about pulling the car up when she froze. That's when her water broke.

* * *

Josh sat in the more comfortable chair of the birthing suite with an ice pack on his head and a spare blanket over him. He'd flat out refused to leave his sister. She was breathing heavy, trying to get her husband to agree to sneaking her a cheeseburger. Tadgh was laughing softly, "Mo chroí, you know that's not allowed. Just have some more broth or Jell-O."

"It's been eight hours since I've eaten, Tadgh O'Brien. Now go get me a freaking cheeseburger before I die of starvation!" Her words escalated to what could only be called a shriek.

Tadgh looked at his Aunt Sorcha who was watching with amusement. "Time to check your progress." They had a doctor on standby, because Charlie wasn't progressing as much as they'd like. Seamus O'Keefe, as a matter of fact. He came in right behind Sorcha. They'd avoid a c-section if they could, but at this point, they'd stopped solid food. Anesthesia and a full belly didn't mix well.

"Do you want me to leave, Sis?" Josh said, but he knew the answer. She gave zero shits about her modesty at this point.

She shook her head, sucking in a breath as the contraction rolled through her. "Just don't look down the gully, and you and I will be able to make eye contact for the next seventy years."

A knock came on the door and Katie smiled as she poked her head inside the room. "How's my girl?" When she saw what they were getting ready to do, she said, "Oops, I'll come back."

The waiting room was full of O'Briens, Murphys, and Donoghues. This family loved a good baby story.

Sorcha checked her cervix as Charlie grimaced. Sorcha smiled with delight. "She's decided to dilate. Nine centimeters and the baby has descended nicely. You're almost there, lass."

Charlie's head fell back on her shoulders. "Thank God. When can I eat?" They all laughed. Charlie's appetite was legendary.

Sorcha said, "You can eat when that babe is out, my love, and no sooner. Now eat your Jell-O and don't say anything you'll regret to my dear nephew. This is getting ready to get exciting and you're going to need him."

* * *

JOSH DIDN'T KNOW how the hell his little sister was doing it, but she rallied for another push. He was off his feet, suddenly stone cold sober and ready to support her. He kissed her sweaty head and thought about their conversation. Would he ever be where Tadgh was? Would he have a wife and child? He thought not. His miserable, albeit brief, encounter with Justine proved that his meter was broken when it came to relationships. A couple of years with the O'Briens wasn't going to undo the first eighteen years of his life. He held his sister's hand while Tadgh held the other. Sorcha motioned to them. "Come see, she's crowning. I see the head!"

"I'll wait for the finale, thanks." Josh really was a modern man, but looking down the gully, as his sister called it, was not in his job description. Tadgh on the other hand whooped as he saw whatever Sorcha was seeing.

"One more push, I think. Maybe two. Are you ready? That cheeseburger is within reach, love." That seemed to rally Charlie.

"I want a double, and I want a milkshake." She ground her molars as she reared up. The push that came out of her was accompanied by a growling scream. The baby came to them, sliding into Sorcha's waiting palms.

"It's a boy! Oh, my darling. He's beautiful!" She held the baby up and Josh's eyes welled up with tears.

"Look what you made, Sis. Jesus, you're a mom." He kissed her hand, so proud and humbled by his strong, beautiful sister.

Charlie was sobbing and so was Tadgh. The nurse helped Sorcha to cut the cord and took the child away to clean him. When she handed the baby to Tadgh, Charlie was delivering the placenta. Then she just watched with sweat covering her reddened face as the love of her life held their son. "William Sean O'Brien."

"Aye, it's good to finally meet you, William. I knew you were a lad. I just knew it." He leaned in and kissed Charlie as she nuzzled her baby. "I'm a happy man. I'm ready to burst from it. Thank you, Charlie. Thank you for our son."

Josh stood by and watched as his Aunt Sorcha worked, and he was amazed by her. She kept her head down, cleaning Charlie up and giving the nurse instructions. Then he saw her eyes. They were full of tears. She dismissed herself, pulling her gloves off as she stifled a sob.

He found her in the hallway, wiping her face. "What is it, Aunt Sorcha? Are you just happy?"

She smiled, swallowing hard. "I delivered Tadgh. Did you know that? I delivered him in this very hospital. He's the child of my heart. My sweetest boy. I helped Katie bring him into the world, then handed him to his father. William was so happy. He thought he'd have a whole life to bring him up, teach him, love him." She started to cry harder and Josh hugged her. She whispered. "I just wish he was here. That's all. The moment I handed his namesake to Tadgh, another healthy boy, I hope he was watching."

"He was. He is, Aunt Sorcha. And now you've made his Katie a grandmother. You did well. Charlie and the baby are both safe."

She smiled at that. "I think Tadgh had more to do with making her a granny than I did." She kissed him on the cheek. Then she touched the small bandage where he'd been struck and then stitched up. "You were a blessing to our family when you came, Josh. A leanbh mo chroí. You're the child of my heart as well. It's not always blood that binds us together. The bonds of love are stronger than even blood ties. Look at wee Estela and Patrick Jr. There's enough love in this family to overshadow any pain that has come before. And the woman who truly wins your heart would never want to see you suffer or deliberately cause you pain. You remember that. You're an O'Brien now, and all of our men eventually find their mates. And the women, come to that. Brigid has Finn. When an O'Brien finds his or her mate, choice or logic has nothing to do with it. It's a pull that won't be denied."

Josh thought about that pull. Damn him, but he'd felt it. He might not be an O'Brien by blood, but he'd felt that pull so strongly he feared it would be his undoing.

* * *

FINN APPROACHED Brigid in the bath, loving the look of her pink skin fresh out of the shower. He took the body oil out of her hand. She used it on her arms and legs to moisturize.

As tantalizing as she was when he watched her rub herself down, he was prepared to do the driving just now. He wrapped his long arms around her and smoothed the oil on her arms as he stood behind her, bringing her sweet body flush against his. When he was done with her arms, and had her panting and pressing against him, he dropped to his knees. He was slow and deliberate as he smoothed the oil up her legs, stopping at the apex of her thighs, refusing to touch her where she wanted.

"Finn, get a condom. I need you." They used the rhythm method for family planning, but this particular time of the month was her fertile time. They had to use a backup method. She was practically moaning as she spoke. He gave a shake of his head as he met her eyes.

"No condom. I want inside." She cried out when he pulled her to his mouth with no warning. He cupped her ass, pulling her against his mouth. He tasted that sweet little nub. "Come, hen. I want to taste it. I want to feel it." He slid a finger inside her as he worked her against his tongue. And she came.

* * *

FINN LAY with Brigid on his chest. They'd been going at it for over an hour. He'd come inside her twice. "I didn't mean to push my agenda on you, love. We should have discussed it first."

"Agenda? You mean the scheme to get a child in me? You like me fat and busty; I think."

His chest rumbled with a husky laugh. "Aye, I do. And I love our children. I love everything you and I have created. Is it okay? Jesus, I'm sorry. I should have discussed it before I…"

She threw a leg over and rose above him. "You mean before you came hard inside me? Twice." She rolled her hips and he was at full salute within seconds. He took her hips, sliding her down on his erection. "Let me tell you something, Finn Murphy. I don't mince words. I'd have told you no if I didn't want this." She started riding him. "So, if we're going to do it, we may as well give it our all."

As he felt their union, he had the absurd urge to cry. He wanted this. A new life growing in her belly. Another beautiful child to love. Colin, Declan, and Cora were everything to him. And there was enough love in this family for a dozen children. An odd thought occurred to him. If it was a girl, he'd call her Miren. After the aunt who had shattered the wall he'd built around himself. His voice was husky as he said, "There's nothing between us, now. I love you, Brigid. I love you so much I think I'll burn up from it." She shrouded him with her auburn hair as she kissed him sweetly. He rose to her mouth, his hair mingling with hers on the stark whiteness of the pillow. He pulled her close, skin to skin, and he felt whole.

CHAPTER 12

DOOLIN, CO. CLARE

inn knocked on the cottage door and walked in when he heard the urgency of his mother's voice. She was helping his Aunt Miren into a chair. "What's this?" He rushed to the other side, holding Miren steady.

When they had her settled, they both sat down at the small kitchen table. Aideen's voice was so thick with emotion it took Finn aback. His mother wasn't one for big displays of emotion. "How long have you been ill, Sister?"

Miren just smiled. "I'm just a bit tired. Don't fret, my dear."

"You're lying to me. I could always tell when you lied, so don't. Please, Miren. I need you to open up to me. I've been noticing how depleted your energy is, especially after working with Cora and Finn."

Finn asked, "Is this true, Auntie? Then why are you doing it? We need to stop!"

She touched his face. "Because, I don't want Cora to be alone in this. Not like I was. Not like you were. We are stronger together. And when I leave this life, you will have each other."

Aideen's eyes welled up, finally understanding. "Are you saying you're terminal, Miren?" When she said nothing, Aideen asked more firmly. "Jesus, when were you going to tell us? How long?" Her voice caught on the words. She waved her hands. "NO! I don't accept this. This isn't right. I need to get you in with a different doctor. Brigid's brother can find someone."

Miren took both her hands and brought them to her lips in a tight bundle and kissed them. "I've had a second opinion." Aideen closed her eyes, shutting out the reality of it all. Miren said softly, "I came here to heal what was wounded."

Aideen's tears were silent. "It was all my fault. You left because of me. We wasted too much time."

"You're wrong, dheirfiúr. I ran from my responsibilities. I was selfish. One of us couldn't have stood up to mother, but together maybe things would have gone differently. We could have made her understand. And I should have stayed for Finn. I was the only one who knew how to help him deal with what was to come. I was his blood. I should have been here to teach him and to protect him. I should have stood with you and helped you understand him." Her eyes welled with tears and they dropped to the top of her sister's hands. "I came here to heal this division. I came here to be in your lives because I was needed here. And I came to say goodbye," She looked at Finn and tears fell silently down his face as well.

He said, "I don't want to lose you a second time. I need you both. I'm not ready, Miren."

She rose and took him in her long, frail arms. He was broad and strong, and she'd missed her nephew so much. She'd been a fool to waste so much time. "No one ever really leaves, my dear lad. And I want you to promise me something. Don't tell anyone else."

Finn stiffened. "I can't keep another secret from Brigid." He spoke in the Irish then. *She's the pulse of my heart.*

She paused, then nodded. "You're right. I won't ask it. But I don't want your sister to know. Colleen is just newly married. This is a happy time for her. And please, Finn, don't tell Cora. I'll know when it's time to tell her, but it must be in my own time."

* * *

FINN WENT BACK to the house to do some work from home. He left the two sisters at the small kitchen table. It was only an hour later when Brigid came into the house digging out a lime from the fridge. "When did you get home?"

"I was flagged down from the drive. Your mother and aunt are on the front porch with their feet up and a drink in their hands." She smiled, saying, "They are doing this retirement thing right."

Curious, he walked out the back door, promising to deliver the lime. His heart squeezed in his chest when he saw them. Big hats, Harry Belafonte playing from an old CD player, and margaritas in their hands. They seemed well in their cups already, despite the lack of a lime.

"Thank you, lad. We're out of lime and Aideen is a drunkard. She wants another pitcher. She's a bad influence altogether." Finn laughed, because his mother never drank more than a sip on special occasions.

"She's a blaggard, my lad. She's stuffing my gob full of tequila like she did when we were twenty." Finn noticed that her words were a little slurred and her smile was huge. And he realized that this was why his aunt had truly come. She'd come to find her sister.

* * *

One Week Later

"Da, Auntie Miren taught me a new trick to try during my dreams. I hope it works next time!" She launched herself into her da's lap and he laughed.

He pushed her dark hair out of her eyes, kissing her between her eyebrows. "Your superpowers are growing, then?"

Cora said, "I don't know. I still can't do the stuff without her with me. She's not allowed to move away."

Finn looked at his aunt, and was sad to see that she was thin and pale. She seemed thinner than at his sister's wedding. "Okay, love. Go help your mother with dinner and we'll have an early night. You have testing tomorrow at school." She kissed him and went off to the kitchen to help her mother.

Miren said, "She's wonderful. I don't have to tell you that. She's emotionally mature for someone so young. More than my last boyfriend." Miren winked and laughed at the look on Finn's face. "What? I'm not dead yet." Then she winced. "Unfortunate choice of words, sorry."

He gave her a chiding look. "How's Mam?"

"Weepy and difficult. She's always been the latter. The former is new. We went to mass together yesterday, though. I think it made her feel better." She clapped her hands. "Now, I promised those handsome boys of yours a round of snakes and ladders before dinner. Don't want to disappoint the lads."

She walked by and Finn took her hand. It was soft for someone who was in her sixties. She had remarkably youthful skin. Still a beauty, just as Cora had said. "I love you, Auntie."

She bent down to kiss him between his dark brows. "And I love you like my own son."

After dinner, Miren went to her cottage. She was overcome with weariness. She just didn't have enough time. But she'd succeeded, for the most part, in setting things to right. And the idea of dragging out her death, weak and in pain, just made her feel even more weary. As she drifted off to sleep, she was content with how her life was ending. No matter how much time she had, she was content and at peace. She smiled as she thought about making Christmas cookies and singing carols with the kids in a few weeks. She'd always loved Christmas. Her mother had been a handful, but she wasn't all bad. She let them string lights through their beautiful garden. They grew mistletoe and herbs and such beautiful flowers. She'd neglected that garden, hadn't she? Sleep claimed her to the smells of the sea air and her childhood home.

* * *

CORA WAS WALKING in a beautiful garden. The flowers were lovely, even at night. The moon shone clear overhead. Her Aunt Miren was bent over a plant, smelling deeply. She picked a small white flower. "What is this place?" Cora looked around, not recognizing it.

"This is my childhood home. It always had such a beautiful garden." She offered the blossom for Cora to smell. "Night blooming jasmine. One of my favorites. I used to sneak out here when the moon was full. I loved the feel of the night air and the smells from our garden. I liked the sounds of the nighttime animals. This place is very special to me. My mother wasn't perfect, but she made our home beautiful and safe. And she had a very green thumb. Just look at the roses." She pointed, as excited as a young girl. "And there's rosemary by the garden gate, just as it should be. It keeps the animals out and is for remembrance of those who have passed." She passed another plant and touched it, saying, "Lavender is for luck and repelling bad things." She smiled at Cora. "It was always such a place of peace for me."

Miren raised her arms up and twirled, her favorite skirt billowing out and around. She giggled, and Cora found herself letting out a little laugh. Her aunt looked like a beautiful, aging witch, dancing before the old Gods.

The sight of her made such affection well up in Cora's chest. Would this be how she would age? She asked, "Why am I in your dream, Aunt Miren? This hasn't happened before. Is it something new I'm to learn?"

Miren put the jasmine flower in her own hair. It was unbound and the streaks of silver hair within the black picked up the light of the moon. She looked more like an angel than a witch, now that Cora thought about it. She answered, finally, because she knew why she'd come here and why she'd pulled Cora along. "Because I thought this was a nice place to show you while it was in its prime. Before time took its toll and neglect made it lose something. Perhaps it will be like this again someday. I brought you here because I have to tell you something. I'm sorry for it, my sweet lass. I've held on as long as I could...taught you as much as I could. I'd stay if I was able. I'd stay with all of you."

Finn smelled something so beautiful, it gave him a spreading sense of comfort deep in his bones. The scent of jasmine was so thick in the air. He loved the scent of earth and grass that accompanied it. But even as he felt that enjoyment and comfort, a deep sadness welled up in his chest. He opened his eyes, and that's when he knew. He put an arm over his eyes and choked down a swell of grief that threatened to overtake him. Then he heard her from down the hall. His little girl let out a sob so mournful it broke down his defenses. "Oh, God. No, Miren. I wasn't ready." His breath stuttered as he lay frozen in this fresh and soul-ripping grief.

Brigid woke up beside him, putting her forehead to the side of his face. She understood. She'd been ready for this, because she knew that Finn would need her. She just hadn't expected it so soon. "I'm sorry, my love. I am so very sorry." Her words were thick with sleep and the creeping tide of tears.

Finn's voice was shaky. "Go to Cora. She shouldn't be alone, and I just need a minute."

Brigid kissed his face, then she rose and ran to Cora's room. His poor Cora knew, even though they'd never told her. Although, he suspected that Miren had finally done so in her own special way.

SEANY AND JOSH put the last piece of furniture in place as they moved into their new home. The Nagles had passed on a gorgeous old farm table, meaning the men had eaten their last meal standing up at the counter. The place was coming along. Josh's head was healing up nicely.

He hadn't seen Madeline since the hospital. He'd been avoiding her without making it obvious. Partly because of the feelings she evoked in him, and partly because he didn't want her to see his head all stitched up. Nine stitches looked a little Frankensteinish and he hated what he'd have to explain. It was going to be hard, though. The stitches weren't due out for a couple more days.

Seany said, "The bachelor pad is finally done. Unfortunately, my time in Dublin isn't over. My shift starts at eleven."

"Yeah, well just be careful. You've only got a few days left in the big city. Then you're a country mouse again. I'll keep working on that interior paint."

"Okay, but you let me know if the RNLI calls you. I like to know where my brothers are. Now, I need a nap." He turned to leave, then stopped. "Tadgh called me. Justine saw the judge and was released for now."

"Yeah, I know. Don't worry. She's not dumb enough to show up here."

"You never know. Just stay sharp, okay. No more excitement is needed in this family." Seany slapped him on the back and headed for his pre-shift nap.

MIREN HADN'T WANTED A FUNERAL, so it was but the work of a couple of days and they were ready to do what had to be done. She hadn't really known how much time she had, but Finn knew her well enough to understand that she did everything on her terms. She hadn't withered away or fizzled out. She'd swept away like an ocean breeze, not making a fuss.

She left a brief will. She split most of her assets between Finn and his sister Colleen with one exception. She still owned the small cottage near the sea which had been her and Aideen's childhood home. It had fallen into a bit of disrepair, but it wasn't unsalvageable. It was just uninhabited at the moment. The cottage was to be held in trust until Cora came of age, then it would be hers. There was a small allotment to maintain the home until Cora turned twenty-five. Finn was to let the home and act as the landlord until Cora decided to live there or sell. Finn knew Cora better than anyone. She'd never sell it. A piece of this small but exciting chapter in her life…and something of her own given by a woman who was a sort of kindred spirit.

It was an odd inheritance for a child of ten. The cottage wasn't valuable. Not near any large cities or very grand, and it was more than a little shabby. The once lovely garden was overgrown and in need of a lot of care. As much of a surprise as it had been, Cora seemed to understand the why of it. After all, Miren had brought her here to say goodbye. Had shown her this special place in it's prime. A glimpse of what it could be again. Only his mother had known. She'd supported the bequest and witnessed the will. After all, Cora was the next generation to carry the torch. The latest in the long lineage of dark Irish who were rumored to descend from the ancient Picts of what was now Scotland. It was certainly no easy torch to carry. Times may have changed. They didn't exactly burn seers at the stake anymore. But Miren had lived a very different sort of life. She had no children or grandchildren of her own. Who better to have this small bit of earth and sky to call her own than Cora?

They stood in the garden now, dormant with winter fast approaching. Miren's ashes were to be scattered in the earth beneath the rose bushes and jasmine vines, and so this small amount of family had gathered to do that very thing. Cora's tears misted on her lashes. She hadn't had much time with her Great-Aunt Miren, but the time they'd spent together would be with her always. And Miren had given her more than her cottage. She'd given her a part of her father which she'd been missing. A piece he'd kept hidden, but now generously shared with his family. His truth, not someone else's secret. That bump in the road had been difficult. But just as with all trials her family faced, the bonds were like that of steel, forged in fire. It was made stronger after the heat and hammering. The pain and suffering. Stronger forever.

Just as Finn began spreading the ashes, a gust of wind blew a portion of them up and overhead, traveling out to the gloomy sea. Aideen said plainly, "She was e'er changing her mind at the last minute." There were a few chuckles, despite the sadness of the day.

Finn added, "And she was meant to be near the sea."

* * *

ONE WEEK later
Doolin, Co. Clare, Ireland

Finn was exhausted. He'd just spent three hours on Cora's math homework. She was a smart lass, but this teacher was a sadist. He drifted off, and his brows furrowed. He smelled something. As he began falling asleep, he recognized it.

He shot out of bed. "Brigid, love. Wake up! I smell smoke."

She was groggy, looking around. "What? Finn, sweetheart, I don't smell anything."

He put some pants on and jerked his door open, checking the hallway. He heard Cora and Genoveva in the living room. When he made an appearance with his eyes wild and his hair unbound, Cora looked at him strangely. "What is it, Da?"

"I smelled something. I thought it was in the house, but I think I was dreaming." Finn scratched his head. "That was just strange. It smelled so real."

"What did you smell?" Cora was afraid to hear the answer. Fear crawled up her spine.

He looked more than a little worried. "I smelled smoke. And I felt heat on my face. I was afraid the house was on fire."

Brigid's phone rang in the bedroom and Cora's eyes grew wide. "Da, something is wrong." Genoveva wasn't sure what was going on, but she kept silent.

Brigid's voice was clipped, and then she became frantic. Finn and Cora ran into the bedroom. "What is it, Mammy?"

Brigid had her hand over her mouth, tears spilling out and down her cheeks. "It's Seany. Dear God, Finn. It's Seany."

EPILOGUE

*S*t. James Hospital
Dublin, Ireland

Josh rubbed his eyes as he leafed through the tradesman text, trying to retain the information about Fresnel lenses in modern lighthouses. Seany was so still, he had to keep watching the monitors and the steady rise of his chest. He was heavily sedated. They'd almost lost him. All of them. And it would have gutted him and destroyed his new family. Seany was the baby, the namesake, the brother and son. The friend. Stupid jackass was too brave for his own good.

He thought about the injuries he'd sustained, and it made his little brush with Justine's beer bottle seem like a scratch. But Seany was young and strong, and considering the condition of the man down the hall, Seany had been extremely lucky.

Sorcha and Sean Sr. had been camping in this room for two days until Liam ordered them to leave and rest at his apartment. The steady flow of O'Briens was constant. But it was two o'clock in the morning right now. They were all resting before they went to work, then they'd flow in again. Many of the women had small children, and they wouldn't let kids back here in the ICU, so they took turns watching each other's babies during visits.

He thought about the oldest O'Brien brother. The fierce warrior, Aidan. Large and commanding and so very stoic. But the first visit to Seany's bedside, the man had wept uncontrollably. He just laid his head down next to his little brother and sobbed without shame until he shook with it. It had been hard to watch. It was an odd thing that the youngest and the oldest seemed to be the closest. But they'd shared some adventures back when Aidan was in America wooing the breathtaking Alanna. His beautiful, kind wife just rubbed his back, weeping silently and letting him tire himself out. It was both heartbreaking and inspiring to see such love between them. He'd only known the O'Brien family for a couple of years, but he loved them with all of his heart. They'd taught him about family. About a father's love. About duty and service. And above all, they'd taught him about the beauty of true love. That it did exist in this harsh world.

He put the book away, knowing it was hopeless. He rose to go to the family courtesy room where he could get a little caffeine and some sort of snack. After grabbing a Coke and something called a Curly Wurly, he started back toward the room. He stopped dead when he saw the figure of a tall, slim woman stalled at the open door of Seany's room. He didn't want to spook her, because she looked very unsure about being there. He just watched. She finally walked in, her long brown braid swinging behind her. She was about his age, maybe a couple years older. She had a pretty profile. Maybe she was an off-duty nurse? Seany was a handsome bastard. Maybe some sort of Florence Nightingale thing was happening?

He decided that creeping on the woman was…well… creepy. He went to the door of the room and she jumped a bit. "It's okay. I didn't mean to scare you. I'm Josh. Are you a friend? I haven't met you before, and I thought I'd met all of the O'Briens."

She smiled, and it was a pretty smile. A subtle, under-stated expression. Serious gray eyes looked at him, as if she was gauging what to tell him. She had dark, sooty lashes. No makeup, but really a very lovely woman. Something niggled at him. She was familiar. She wasn't actually that tall, now that he was closer. Her lithe body and long limbs made her appear taller than she was. He was surprised to see she was wearing cowboy boots. You didn't see them very often in Ireland.

She finally said, "I'm an old friend. I mean… I was a friend. It's been a while."

"You're American," he said dumbly. She didn't reply. Her eyes combed over Seany's face and body, like she was reac-quainting herself with the sight of him. He saw longing and old pain in her eyes. Something he understood. *American*…he knew she was someone significant. Then it hit him. The photos in Seany's teenage photo albums. And a few which Alanna had shown him when Seany seemed to not want to talk about the young woman who he'd spent a summer with in America.

He spoke softly. "You're her." She cocked her head, not understanding him. "You're Moe."

She stiffened. Then she put her hands in the pockets of her jeans. "I just wanted to see he was alive and well. That's all. Thank you, Josh. I'm exhausted. I took the red-eye when I found out, yesterday. I'll say goodnight." She turned and saw Seany was stirring, trying to wake from the fog of pain meds. She walked toward the door and said, "Please, don't tell him I was here. He wouldn't thank you for it. I'm asking this for his sake, not mine. Please don't tell him I was here."

Seany groaned, and Josh turned to him for a brief moment. When he looked back at the doorway, the young woman was gone.

AUTHOR NOTES AND
ACKNOWLEDGEMENT

I hope you enjoyed this latest in the long and beautiful story of the O'Brien family. Brigid and Cora have been a consistent favorite for fans of the series. Finn has been a constant and stable presence, always in the background, but just as beloved and significant to this family. But I scratched beneath the surface, and Finn had his own story to tell us. As with all of my books, it wasn't just about the primary couple. The O'Brien Tales are an intricately woven tapestry. *Dark Irish: An O'Brien Novella,* was not just about Finn and his family. The rest of the beloved O'Briens, Mullens, Murphys, and Nagles are living their own lives, and it's fun to sneak a peek at what everyone is doing. New jobs, new babes, new heartbreaks. And as you now know, there's a bit of a cliffhanger. Stay tuned, because these stories aren't over. I have several books in the works and will continue to let the O'Brien family and their friends lead me on this ever changing journey to find their mates.

I've had the pleasure of traveling to Ireland three times. Twice, I have been drawn up the Wild Atlantic Way to the unspoiled coves and cliffs of Donegal. It's in that untamed land that Ireland speaks to me most clearly. Everything is a bit wilder. The flowers and the spongey feel of the turf under your feet. The wind carrying the sound of sheep instead of people. It's also the birthplace of our beloved Granny Aoife. Along the way we drove through the charming university town and well known bays of Galway. Full of tourists, good seafood, and pubs full of music. Good craic, to be sure. Sean Jr. and Josh are on their own paths, starting careers and dealing with the growing pains of young men. They both whisper to me in those moments when I'm supposed to be sleeping, nudging me to tell their tales. And I will.

The Royal National Lifeboat Institution is a non-profit, volunteer organization in the U.K. and Ireland which help with search and rescue/recovery in the waters surrounding those island countries. As we discussed in Raven of the Sea: An O'Brien Tale, the Irish Coastguard is almost all volunteer. So, you can see why the RNLI is so very crucial during a crisis. It's not everyone who will stand up and be called when the seas are rough and tragedy strikes. Their motto is: *With courage, nothing is impossible.*

Made in the USA
Las Vegas, NV
02 March 2023

68396589R00095